The
Celestial Bar

The Celestial Bar

A Spiritual Journey

Tom Youngholm

Delacorte Press

Published by
Delacorte Press
Bantam Doubleday Dell Publishing Group, Inc.
1540 Broadway
New York, New York 10036

Author: Tom Youngholm with Mike MacCarthy
Cover Design: Tom Youngholm
Illustrated: GraphiComm
Creative Book Design Consultant: Dianne Sala

Library of Congress Cataloging in Publication Data
Youngholm, Tom.
    The celestial bar: a spiritual journey / Tom Youngholm.
      p.   cm.
    ISBN: 0-385-31548-1
    I. Title.
    PS3575.08693C45   1995   95-11706
    813' .54—dc20   CIP
                                                         AC

Reprinted by arrangement with Creative Information Concepts
Manufactured in the United States of America
Published simultaneously in Canada
10 9 8 7 6 5 4 3 2 1
BVG

To My Friends

Who have always encouraged and believed in me.

I count myself in nothing else so happy
As in a soul remembering my good friends.

Shakespeare, *"Richard II"*

Acknowledgments

I wish to thank Mike MacCarthy for helping me with the "design" of my words. Thanks to Lianne Stevens Downey for her guidance and fine tuning, Dave Peters and Mark Bowers for their computer expertise. Many thanks to Karen Popowski, Bob, Debbi, and Jake Gillespie, Diane Doyle, Pam Iverson, Gayle Watson, "Kat" Edwards, and Dianne Sala for all of their informative and insightful feedback.

Thanks to Ahmay, Mark, Ramda, Zorinthalian, and Paula. Without their wisdom, patience, and love, all of this would not be possible.

To all of you who have helped me along this journey: Thanks.

Author's Note

Throughout most of my life, the challenging and even the happier times, I felt that something was missing. I didn't know what it was, just that I didn't have it. One day in February of 1987 while meditating, I drifted off to a place ... a place beyond the walls of my memory. Over the next seven years, people, places, books, movies, geometric shapes, and music triggered a knowingness within me that was outside my apparent life experiences. After recording as much as I could remember, I have written this novel in an attempt to reconstruct my journey—my visit to ... ?

Many of the characters, places, and events in *The Celestial Bar* have actually occurred in my life; I've changed some names to allow privacy. This book weaves a story that flows between the many realities of my consciousness. I now know they actually exist. To perceive these new realities, all it took was for me to change my focus. Then, I saw myself as being of spirit on a homeward journey, and that realization enabled me to walk my path in love and to more fully understand this world with all its joys, sufferings, and complexities; it was then that peace and balance began to find a more permanent presence within me. But it all began with my spirituality: my recognition of its essential role, and my willingness to take action on this new focus.

The purpose of *The Celestial Bar* is to share my journey in hope that all of you will experience this exciting, wondrous, and loving new world with me. I know now all of us occasionally need directions, rest, nourishment, and friendship. Remember, none of us are alone in this quest. So if you're feeling an empty aching in your heart or a missing "something," drop in at my favorite place: The Celestial Bar.

Hope to see you there,

Tom

October 1994

Prologue

"He didn't know what it was, but he was looking for something more in his life."

San Diego

Digger suddenly felt cold as the wind blew through his body. He had the feeling that someone was following him, as he looked back over his shoulder. He stood before the apartment complex that he lived in many years ago, when his dad died. More frightened than confused, he quickly began the ascent to his third-floor apartment. As he turned the knob to his front door, he sensed that this unknown assailant might already have entered his private domain—the one place in his life where he'd felt in control. The door swung wide, carrying Digger inside. He found himself standing in the middle of his living room with a fear of impending doom. The air got thicker as the temperature rapidly decreased. A feeling of lightness came to his body. He noticed with utter amazement that he was no longer standing on the floor but somehow was suspended in mid-air. The next moment he was flung through the air. He heard and felt each of his ribs crack as they slammed against the mantle of the fireplace. As his body slumped to the ground, he tasted the saltiness of his own blood from an open gash above his right eye.

Again, the invisible force threw his body against the walls as if he were a human pinball. With extreme clarity,

Digger felt every broken bone, laceration, and contusion. He prayed that he'd lose consciousness—that it would all go away. Lying on the floor like a human rag doll, he felt the presence of someone standing over him. He strained to see who it was, but blood streamed down his face and into his eyes, not allowing a clear vision of his tormentor. Digger gave up. He couldn't fight this overwhelming force.

"It is time," someone yelled off in the distance.

The attacker's attention was momentarily diverted as the same voice repeated, "It is time."

Digger felt his body being effortlessly picked up by this unknown force and then thrown through the window.

"Digger, it's time," said a familiar voice. "What the hell are you doing?"

Digger Taylor shivered and looked around. All his teammates in the dugout were staring at him. He'd been daydreaming, thinking about the nightmare he'd had again last night.

"Come on, Digger," said Hank Olsen, the team captain and second baseman. He picked up Digger's glove and flipped it to him, "Last inning. We're down one. Come on. Let's hold'em."

Digger caught his glove and jogged out into the mid-morning sunlight, onto the dirt infield.

"At the end of eight innings complete here at Presidio Park," barked the P.A. system, "the score is Black Angus, eight; Harbor Cafe, seven. For those of you witnessing your first slow-pitch championship game, we do it here just like they do in the 'bigs': if the score is tied at the end of nine innings, we keep going until someone is ahead at the completion of a full inning."

Can't believe you were daydreaming like that, Digger thought to himself while he took warm-up ground balls from the first baseman. It's bad enough most everyone on this team thinks you're kind of strange. Now they're going to think you don't even give a damn—daydreaming in the middle of a championship ball game. What the hell's wrong with you, Taylor?

He really wanted to be a part of the team—a part of anything. He'd felt disconnected for so long that it was hard for him to get out of his cocoon. This was not the time to be unfocused. He had to do something that showed he really cared.

No one on the team had been able to figure him out. He told them his nickname had been Digger since high school because of his ability to "dig out" ground balls and run fast, but they suspected the name meant more than that. He always had his nose stuck in some library book about music composition or philosophy. Lately—when he wasn't playing his piano—he'd even tried some "California kinds of things," like meditation and yoga. He didn't know what it was, but he was looking for something more in his life.

The only thing his teammates knew for sure was that Jonathan Patrick Taylor was the best damn shortstop in the Restaurant Softball League and they were glad to have him. The umpires said Digger was one of the top softball players in the county; everyone wondered why he wasn't playing professionally.

At the Harbor Cafe, none of his fellow employees could understand why Digger worked as a waiter. He looked only slightly older, but it was obvious he knew more about running a restaurant than the managers or the chef or even the owner. Still, he just kept to himself—came early, left late, and busted butt. His employment application listed only a P.O. box at the central post office.

"Batter up," bellowed the plate umpire.

The first batter hit a hot smash to the third baseman. With long surfer hair blowing in his eyes, the fielder made the play cleanly and threw to first. "Out," barked the base umpire on a bang-bang play. The stands erupted with cheers and applause. The crowd began to chant "Defense! Defense!"

The P.A. announced that the next batter was a pinch hitter.

"This guy hits to the right side," Digger yelled over at Olsen as he moved toward second. "I played against him once in a traveling league; he swings inside-out."

Olsen moved closer to first and signaled for the center fielder to move to his left. The outfielder moved one step.

First pitch, the batter hit a "rope" to right center. It rolled to the fence and the batter loped into third, standing up.

Digger took the throw from the outfield and held onto the ball; there was no play at third. He called "time" and walked the ball toward the pitcher.

Olsen motioned for the infielders to join him in a conference at the mound. "What do you think, Digger?" he asked once everyone was there. "Everyone should play in, right?"

Digger nodded. "We've got a fast runner at the plate, but let's remember to try and hold the runner at third."

The others nodded in agreement and jogged back to their positions.

The next batter was a short, thin man whose baseball cap almost obscured his chalky face.

The infielders hunched low and even with the nearest base, waiting to move with the pitch. The pitch lofted high in the air and descended almost straight down near the plate. The batter didn't move; neither did Digger nor the rest of the infielders.

"Ball one," bellowed the umpire.

Again the next pitch was lofted high in the air. For some reason, Digger had already started running toward the plate. The batter over-swung and lifted a soft, low arching pop-up, near the third base line. The runner broke toward home as soon as the bat met the ball.

Digger knew if the ball hit the ground in fair territory and stayed fair, the runner would score because the third baseman couldn't get to the ball in time to make a play at home. Like a blur out of nowhere, he dove through the air and caught the ball before it hit the ground. He landed on the dirt infield, sliding hard on his stomach. Almost before he came to a stop, he jumped to his feet and threw to the third baseman, who caught it and stepped on the bag.

"Out on the catch!" yelled the umpire. "And out at third."

The crowd leaped to their feet, clapping and cheering.

"Nice play, Digger," muttered the third base coach as Digger jogged past him toward the third base dugout.

"Thanks," Digger said, shaking his right hand in pain. He looked at his pinkie finger. It was pointing out at a forty-five degree angle. Already the finger was discolored and swollen.

Not now, Digger thought, not now. I've got too much to do. A thin veil of despair clouded over him.

"What's the matter laddie?" Digger heard some loudmouth with an Irish accent yell from beyond the outfield fence. "Gotta go home and have yer mum fix yer little fingy?"

Digger scowled and strained to see the man but couldn't pick him out. He felt a chill.

Chapter 1

"Love ... requires care and nurturing."

San Diego, Four Months Later

As Digger pedaled his bike, he felt the cool Pacific breeze against his face. He rode along the boardwalk where there were usually lots of people on skateboards, Rollerblades, walking, or jogging. But at three in the morning it was quiet. Digger loved the nighttime; there were no distractions, no places to go, no chores to do. This was the time when he was most introspective and creative. It was the time of day that most reflected how he felt inside.

When he reached the breakwater at the foot of Mission Beach, he put his bicycle down and locked it up. He climbed over several rocks as he made his way out to the tip of the jetty. Rarely was there anyone else out there at that time of night. He slid on one of the slippery rocks and put his hand out to protect his fall. He had to be more careful, he thought. Can't break any more fingers. His broken pinkie had already cost him valuable composing time. His finger was just about healed, but it would usually cramp up when he reached a particular phrase in the concerto he was trying to finish.

As usual, he'd gotten off work from the restaurant about one in the morning and gone home to work on his music. But he couldn't get in the creative mood, so he had decided to go for a bike ride. There was so much going on in his head: paying off his bills, finishing his concerto, dealing with his feelings about Mary, getting a real job— and then there was that nightmare he kept having over and over again. A familiar feeling of emptiness was also starting to creep over him during the last several months. From previous experience, he knew that meant trouble was on the horizon.

He sat there for about an hour, watching the waves lap over the rocks just a few feet below him. He looked out to the west, with the city lights behind him, because it was the best for star-gazing. The stars were so much clearer out here. He could sit for hours and just let his mind go. The sky would stir his imagination and the sea would somehow soothe his heart.

But an uneasy feeling that someone was following him swept through him again. He rationalized that his fear must be stemming from his nightmares. But lately, he was beginning to feel as if someone in his waking world was following him.

He got up and walked back towards the boardwalk. Out of the corner of his eye, he thought he saw a shadowy figure. That would be impossible. Nobody else was out there with him; he was sure of that. Nonetheless, he quickened his pace. He got to his bike and spun the dial on his lock. A rock tumbled down the side of the jetty and fell into the water. Digger looked but didn't see anyone. He turned back to his lock but couldn't remember the last digit.

Come on Digger, he thought, get your head together. A little panic and you fall apart. It came to him—eighteen. He slid the lock through the spokes and quickly began to pedal.

Once he was over the bridge, the fear finally dissipated. He wanted to be around some people. He rode to his favorite late-night hangout.

The clock on the wall in the Hardee's on Voltaire and Sunset Cliffs read 4:35 a.m. Dressed in a brown, A–line uniform, Mary Porcelli swished out of the ladies room, strutting her curvaceous twenty–eight-year-old body. Her long, brown hair was neatly brushed and tied in a bun under the required hairnet, her makeup and lipstick freshly applied to a stunning face.

From booths just outside the restrooms, piercing catcalls and whistles greeted her entrance. "Whee doggies," shouted Zippo, a heavyset biker with a long beard and massive bare arms covered with tattoos. The assembled early morning crowd howled with laughter. Most were regulars who worked irregular shifts or couldn't think of anything better to do at this hour of the morning.

"You'd better watch out, Zippo," Mary snapped over her shoulder.

"Ohhhh," chorused the group, sensing some excitement. Something was wrong; she wasn't usually so touchy.

Mary had a lot on her mind. She couldn't wait to get through with school and get her teaching credentials. This job had helped her pay for her tuition and still go to school during the day. But it was Digger who had been on her mind the last few weeks.

"Where's your buddy, Mary?" asked a cabby—one of the regulars.

Mary knew whom he was talking about, but decided not to answer. She slipped behind the counter and went back to cleaning. She didn't want to upset Jake, the night manager. Trading verbal barbs with customers was one of his pet peeves. Besides, she wanted to get in some brownie points for when Digger finally did decide to show.

Once behind the counter, no one from the "over–the–hill–gang"—that's what Jake called them—dared hassle any of his help. They were already on pretty shaky ground with him anyway, especially when Digger wasn't there.

Just then Digger walked in, pushing his bike. Sweat covered his body. His friends broke into spontaneous applause.

"Nice of you to join us," barked Zippo. "Where the hell ya been for the last few days?"

"Just around."

"Digger," ordered the cabby, "sit here. I need your opinion about a business situation."

Digger grinned. "Sure, but can I order some food first?"

With a quick glance, Digger got Mary's attention and gave her hand signals for coffee and something hot to eat.

The short stocky man proceeded to tell Digger about an insurance problem he was having with his cab business.

For several minutes, Digger went into great detail about all the advantages and disadvantages of his friend's insurance options. He thought to himself, how ironic; I'm the last person on Earth anyone should ask for advice on insurance, considering the way I bungled it in Florida.

Many of the group were shaking their heads in admiration at Digger's knowledge and understanding of the problem.

The biker said, "Where'd you learn that shit, Taylor? Are you some kinda lawyer or somethin'?"

Digger chuckled good–naturedly. "No lawyer," he answered. "Cruel, hard experience is how you learn that stuff."

As he finished, Mary brought a tray with hot coffee, milk, an omelet, and a sweet roll to go in a bag. "Sure got quiet in here all of a sudden," she said, an impish grin on her face. "What's going on? You guys planning to break the bank at Las Vegas or something?"

"Nothing like that, but it certainly would help me out," Digger said, smiling and looking up into her soft brown eyes. He loved to look at Mary. Besides being beautiful, she had many of the qualities he thought he was looking for in a woman: intellect, humor, drive, thoughtfulness, independence, and a little sassiness.

He reached for his money to pay her. "Just a little business problem," he continued, "but if we do figure out how to beat the house in Las Vegas or any place else, believe me, you'll be among the first to know. Then you can quit working all the crazy hours you work in this place."

He found his money and dropped a ten–dollar bill on the tray. "Tell me, Mary, what would you do if you went to Las Vegas and won $100,000?"

She raised her eyebrows and shrugged. Her smile disappeared and she stared out into the darkness. "I don't know. Pay some bills. Finish my degree. Buy a house. Travel, maybe. I think I'd like to go visit Rome. I've … " She caught herself, began to blush, looked quickly back at the faces of the group, and then down at her tray. "I'll be right back with your change."

Digger opened the paper bag and checked its contents. Sometimes Mary slipped him a note. Sure enough. He saw the note and palmed it.

"Nature calls," he announced, getting up and heading for the men's room. Once in a stall, he read Mary's familiar handwriting: "I need to talk to you."

Good grief, he thought, why can't she just leave it alone? He didn't want to deal with this issue—mostly because he didn't know what to say to her.

Mary and Digger had dated five or six times, but that had ended about a month ago. The relationship had gone fairly well, but he didn't want to set himself up for another failure. He never really opened up to her, and she sensed the walls closing around him. He told her that he wasn't ready.

Truthfully, Digger could not come up with any rational reason why he shouldn't be madly in love with her. All he could think of was to tell her, "It's not you, dear, it's me." And that was the truth. It was him. He just didn't know what "it" was. All he knew was that something was missing in his life.

In the summertime, lifeguard tower number seventeen in Ocean Beach—or OB, as the locals called it—was usually crowded with activity from mid–morning until well after sunset. At dawn, though, there was usually no one around except sea gulls and the wind and the roar of the pounding surf.

This morning, Mary was leaning against the tower waiting for Digger, watching the colors of a new day's light paint the sea. She'd undone her brown hair. Long, thick locks hung down from inside the hood of her white sweatjacket. Her arms were crossed impatiently.

She'd liked Digger from the first night he had come in the restaurant. He walked with an air of self-confidence, but most of all, there was a kindness in his smile. Then there was his aura of mystery. It was a double-edged sword—it intrigued but it also excluded her. Digger was a very private person who didn't share much information. In fact she had never even been to his place. Her girlfriends told her that he was probably dating someone else. She didn't want to believe them.

Mary also sensed a pain somewhere within Digger that she wanted to take away but knew she couldn't. "Rescuing" was one of her old habits in relationships; she definitely wanted to break it. Deep inside, though, she felt there was hope for them. She didn't know how to get through to Digger, but she wanted to give it one last try.

Digger finally appeared, pushing his bike through the sand toward Mary. "Sorry it took me so long," he apologized. "Zippo is determined to teach me to ride his Harley. I don't think he understands the word 'no.'"

A good–natured smile covered Mary's face. "No problem," she said, taking a deep breath. "You know, he worships you, Digger. You're like a god to him. You'd make him the happiest man in OB if you ever let him teach you to ride that thing."

"I think you're probably right," Digger agreed. "That's what scares me." He leaned the bike up against the tower and turned to face her. "So ... what's up?"

11

She briefly closed her eyes. "Come on, Digger. Don't give me that wide–eyed, innocent look. You know perfectly well what's on my mind."

He shrugged. "Well, I've got an idea. But I never really know for sure, Mary."

"Digger, what do I have to do? I've done everything but throw myself at you. What does it take to get through to you? You'd been coming to the restaurant for a year before you had the nerve to ask me out. And then, when we finally did go out, it was wonderful. You even said so yourself. Then all of a sudden you retreat."

"I don't know what to say." He hung his head. How can I explain it to her when I don't understand it myself? That emptiness always crept into him, whether it was in relationships, careers, or new cities, that feeling that there had to be more—not just a little more, but a Grand Canyon more. And lately that feeling had been growing.

"What's the problem?" Mary continued, "Why aren't we making love some place, or sound asleep right now in each other's arms? You know that I really care for you and I think you feel the same way. What are you waiting for?"

"I thought I'd explained it to you," he said, playing coy.

"Digger! The only thing you've said is that you're not ready. That doesn't explain anything."

He took a deep breath, cleared his throat, and began pacing. All he could really tell her were the things that made sense to his rational mind:

"I came to San Diego four years ago, leaving behind a series of failed relationships in Florida. Before that, I'd done the same thing in Chicago, only then it involved marriage and divorce. I made up my mind that when I moved here, I had to get my head together before I got involved with anyone else.

"So ... for the last three years that's what I've been working on. I don't have another girlfriend or a boyfriend or any addictions. I do one thing. I write music. That's it ... end of big picture."

She frowned. "That's it? That's all you do?"

"That and play a little softball."

"What kind of music?"

"Concert music for piano and orchestra."

"You do? All this time and you've never mentioned it?"

Digger shrugged.

Mary just looked at him, realizing she'd fallen in love with a man she knew almost nothing about. It didn't make sense.

"Can I hear you play some day?" she asked softly. Gone was the critical edge, replaced now by admiration and surprise.

"Someday ... I don't have any music yet that's ready for prime time. But I'm getting close ... well, closer, maybe."

"What kind of an answer is that?"

There was a brief silence while he thought. Sea gulls squawked high above.

"A crummy answer." he said finally. His words were quiet and wistful. "But it's a truthful one, too. I don't feel good enough about my work to show it off yet. Until then, I don't have the time or the energy for anyone or anything else. I'm sorry." He paused, looking at her beautiful features in the golden sunrise. "Is that clear enough?"

She studied him, then just nodded. "Clear enough," she said gently, eyes blinking. "Remember one thing, Piano Man. She may be crazy, but Mary Benedetta Porcelli loves you ... a lot. While you're hiding behind your music, you're the loser. Love is not like a weed that will grow by itself. Love is like a beautiful and sensitive flower: it requires care and nurturing."

Mary reached into her pocket and pulled out a small envelope. "This is my new address and phone number. Tonight was my last night at Hardee's. When you're ready for a real life, give me a call. I hope our flower is still alive and strong."

She pecked him on the cheek and walked across the white, drifting sands.

Chapter 2

"Something was missing; he couldn't figure out what."

The sun was beginning to warm the city as Digger rode down the driveway, past a house, to a small, one-bedroom cottage. Nearby the surf moaned and crashed to shore. That was the main reason he'd chosen this place: proximity to the ocean. The sounds and smells of the sea had always pulled him near.

He also liked the privacy of the place—not only for himself, but he could play his music without bothering anyone. And the price was right. After all, where else in San Diego but Ocean Beach could he find a one bedroom within spitting distance of the surf for only five hundred a month?

He certainly needed to save every cent. He was still paying off loans to his mom and a friend. In fact, the IRS was making all kinds of threats because he still hadn't made the final balloon payment on his overdue taxes. His failed endeavor in Florida was still haunting him—in many different ways.

Digger turned the key in the lock and opened the door to his cottage. He took a deep breath, sighing to himself as he closed the door. Home sweet home, he thought.

He was never going to get this thing done without discipline. Maybe today things would be different. He was tired of this business of working hour after hour, day after day, week after week, with little music to show for all his trouble. Maybe Mother was wrong. Maybe he didn't have that much talent after all.

He tossed his keys on the kitchen table and walked over to the empty fridge. Then he saw the teeming black spots. He hadn't washed dishes in days; swarms of ants covered the pots, plates, and glasses.

What the heck, he thought, they aren't hurting anything. At least he'd remembered to cover the peanut butter and jelly. When you're out of "peannie–boo and j," you're out of food. That's what his dad used to say when he'd come home late, looking for a snack.

The ants reminded Digger of another time and place, and he chuckled to himself. Judy, his old partner in Florida, had a favorite saying about ants: "Everybody's got to be someplace, eh mate?" she'd say, a cheery grin spread across her handsome Australian face. "Just as long as they're outside."

I'll clean the ants up later, he thought. He was preoccupied by everything Mary had just said to him. Preoccupied and disturbed.

He went over to his bureau where jeans and old T–shirts were piled high. He changed his clothes, and opened the cottage windows. A gentle spring breeze wafted in, bringing with it the smells of the sea. Digger took a deep breath.

He started to pass by the piano, but turned and with his right hand began to play some notes. It was a reflex action for Digger, like trying to pass a candy jar: once he'd noticed it, he just had to have a taste.

From the corner of one eye, he noticed a pair of shorts covering his answering machine. The machine had been a Christmas present from his mother. She wanted him to know whenever she called and he wasn't there. "I can't keep up with your crazy schedule," she'd said. He'd remembered that he really hadn't checked his machine in a couple of days. He removed the shorts, exposing a blinking light.

Out of habit, he hit the "Play" button. A piercing chill coursed through his body.

"Hello, Patrick? Sean Green here," came a lilting Irish brogue from the machine.

Digger rolled his eyes to the ceiling and shook his head. Who could mistake that voice? His agent—the agent he'd never even met—was the only person in the world who called him by his middle name.

"Haven't heard from ya in a while," continued Green. "Need to hear how your concerto's coming, ya know. Gave your tape of the first movement to some big folks. Don't let me down, now. Gave 'em my word, I did. Told 'em you'd be having it done any day. Ring me up and tell me if I've made a mistake. Ya know the number." He hung up.

Several months ago Digger had sent out some audio tapes of his music to several agents on the West Coast. Green was the only one who had expressed any interest. Periodically he would call to see how Digger was progressing. Digger knew he should be thankful, but there was something about the guy he didn't like.

Digger sat down at the piano, still shaking his head. The top of the instrument and the music holder were cluttered with piles of manuscript paper filled with notes and scribbled ideas. Line after line of different key signatures covered the sheets—he'd been experimenting with varying counterpoints.

For a moment, he studied the old Clark and Player upright. He'd bought it at a garage sale the first week he'd moved to San Diego. It was scarred with scratches from decades of abuse, but it was the only thing he could afford. He spent several weeks refinishing it. Now it looked just like his mother's old piano—the one thing she really ever cared about. She'd raised hell so her husband would buy her new furniture and carpeting and appliances, but her piano was all that really mattered to her. When Digger was about ten, she told him that the piano was the only thing her father had let her take when she left home to raise her own family. Grandpa Leahy didn't want his daughter marrying some uneducated factory worker; that's not why he sent her through college and graduate school, he'd rant and rave.

To please his mother was the only reason Digger had taken piano lessons in the first place. It certainly hadn't been his intention to spend all those hours practicing when he could have been playing Little League baseball or Pop Warner football or YMCA basketball.

At first he hated playing the piano. Being brought up in an Irish Catholic neighborhood, his mother had sent him to the nuns for his lessons. Digger remembered his knuckles being hit by a pointer because he had "slouching fingers." The nuns stressed playing technique, but Digger knew there was much more to music than finger technique. In one of his few acts of defiance as a child, he finally refused to play at all. His mother, in an act of desperation, made a pact with little Jonathan: she would honor his request if he would just play for three more months under a new teacher—one who was not a nun.

Within the first two weeks, Digger discovered what music was really about. The new teacher exposed him to different kinds of music and made it fun to play. He couldn't express it in words at that young age, but as an adult, Digger knew that playing the piano was a way of expressing all the emotions that were caught up inside him.

Emotions had been very confusing to the young Jonathan. He was frightened by his mother's strong emotions. (So were his friends, who avoided coming to his house if they could.) Mrs. Taylor was a well-intentioned woman who wanted the best for her son, but she had great difficulty in dealing with the unpredictable behavior of a young boy. She attempted to control him by yelling and screaming. But whenever Digger showed his own emotions of displeasure or anger, his mother was quick to squelch them by "washing his mouth out" with soap.

On the other hand, Digger's father was a very quiet and gentle man, one who held his emotions in check— especially anger. His dad was always working. When he did come home, he would always grab a beer and go to the "rec" room to watch TV. An argument would usually begin—his mom yelling and his dad sitting there quietly.

In an unconscious decision, Digger had followed his father's path of keeping it all inside. But playing the piano allowed him to express the full range of emotions in a safe and acceptable form.

Both his parents had found ways to work longer and harder so that Digger could have better and better music instructors. By the time he was in Catholic high school, he'd won several competitions and had been courted by many of the best music schools in the Chicago area. His knowledge, technique, and passion had grown tremendously through his college years.

Everything changed, though, after he graduated from college.

In his junior year, Digger studied in Europe. During that time, his father, who had been a heavy drinker, fell seriously ill from the extensive damage done to his liver and brain. By the time Digger came back to Loyola University for his final year, his father was doing much better.

The doctors, whom Digger usually held in contempt for their drug approach to every problem, were very straightforward with his father. They told him if he started to drink again, it would kill him.

That's when Digger felt a strong urge to get closer to his dad. Neither of them had ever been deep-sea fishing, so he worked extra hours and planned a surprise vacation to Key West for the two of them. It had been many years since just the two of them had been together—that was when he was a little boy at Shawano Lake.

Digger still couldn't remember all the details of that Florida vacation. He did know that his dad started drinking again. When he reminded his father of the doctor's warning his father's only reply was, "I know exactly what I'm doing."

His father's cold statement of self-destruction left Digger paralyzed. He wanted to tell his father how much he loved him, how much he wanted to ease his pain, but Digger couldn't say anything; couldn't do anything. He just stood there. Digger knew so little about his father, who kept so much bottled up inside.

After they came home from Florida, Digger's musical interest rapidly declined. It dissipated totally a few months later when his father died.

A wave crashed down on the beach outside and brought Digger back to the present. "There you go again depressing yourself," he said out loud. He stood up from the piano stool and kicked the crumpled music sheets on the floor to one side.

He thought about his love/hate relationship with this instrument. He loved the playing but hated how he couldn't capture on paper all the notes he heard and felt inside.

Digger turned his attention back towards the keyboard. He took a deep breath and tried to let go of his mind. You've got work to do, he told himself. You haven't written any new music worth keeping in days; the least you can do is run through the first and second movements, just to warm up. Who knows what might happen after that? He sat down at the piano and rubbed his hands together.

When he could totally let go, it was magical. He could leave behind the mundane and the real and enter his own special world of creation, where he was master of all he surveyed, the moving force for his own universe. Here, he was truly free. Here, he was at another level of reality—a consciousness of empowerment. Here, he tasted the array of emotions long fermenting within the dark cellars of his heart.

Playing his music was somehow treading on the road to fulfillment. He wasn't there yet, but something told him that he was on the right path. The key somehow was the music. No, he thought for a moment, music was only the door. The key was this piece of music, this concerto that had been dancing in his head his whole life.

He knew that concertos did not have transitions from one movement to the next, but somehow his concerto needed one. He could hear the imaginary ridicule of his teachers: "Mr. Taylor, what you are trying to accomplish is not possible. Concertos simply do not have transitions." But his concerto did.

Somewhere within him, he could hear those transitional notes; he could feel the connection. He just couldn't get it out.

His fingers barely touched the stained ivory keys, almost as if he were about to make love with a highly sensuous woman. He felt the titillation racing through his arms and limbs till he could no longer wait.

He began to play, slowly and gently at first. That's how he'd written the opening: *pianissimo*. The music reminded him of the sadness he felt about his life. The humiliation of so many failures amid what he thought was a life brimming with promise. That's what made him feel so sad: he was always going to be; he never was—so much potential, so little accomplishment.

Now came the anger. *Crescendo.* His penchant for not leaving situations till they were forced on him: the broken marriage and weekend nightmare in Chicago—senseless accidents that almost cost him his life; the stupidity of Florida—the failed restaurant and relationship with Judy. Then leaving his career as a family counselor for the Sheriff's Department in Chicago and now not being able to find a job except where he worked for tips. A master's degree in Human Relations and his career move as he approached forty was more of the same: waiting tables. The irony of it defied explanation. No matter how he tried, no matter how much education he had, or where he lived, he couldn't distance himself from the restaurant business.

He'd finally decided to use this downtime in his career to rediscover his music. The idea lately had been bearing fruit. When he had called his mother and played the new composition for her over the phone, her voice cracked with joy. That was before he broke his little finger.

His pinkie missed a note. It had cramped up again at the exact place in the transition as last time, and the time before that. This was getting to be a bad habit.

Digger had gone to the doctors several times to see what could be done. As far as they could tell, his finger had totally healed. All they could do was to prescribe drugs—muscle relaxers.

Like the professional he had trained himself to become, he smoothly segued to the next melody interline. An uninformed listener would never have known.

Why do you let yourself think about that stupid softball accident, dummy?

He stopped playing and shook his right hand. The cramp went away, but the mood had been broken. "Damn," he yelled into the empty room, pounding a fist into his thigh. "I'm tired of this crap!" He stood up and, with one sweep of his hand, knocked all the sheet music from the piano onto the floor. "This is insanity. I hate it."

Digger cleaned the cottage. He knew he'd feel better once he got something accomplished, even if it was only that. He tried to decide what was blocking him from Mary while he hummed the transition between the first and second movements, over and over. The whole concerto seemed dead. Something was missing; he couldn't figure out what.

Chapter 3

"It'll come back to ya ... "

Digger felt his body being effortlessly picked up by an unknown force. Then he began to fly through the air. The next instant his body smashed through his apartment window. He felt each and every one of the shards of glass explode within him as he hit the pavement three stories below. He couldn't believe he wasn't dead. He wished he were; at least the pain would stop. Through swollen eyes, he saw a dark shadow covering his body. A feeling of total resignation overwhelmed him. He waited for the final blow; it would carry him away from all this pain.

It began to rain and his senses became more lucid. Now he was running. The shadowy figure was behind him and catching up with every step.

"It is time, Jonathan," said a voice through the driving rain. Digger saw a light coming from a building in the distance. He ran faster with every new step. Then a heavy hand grabbed his shoulder and brought him to a halt. As he turned around, he let out a scream ...

Digger bolted straight up from the chair, beads of sweat dripping from his temples. Damn it, this has to stop, he thought to himself; his heart was still pounding in his chest. When was this dream ever going to end?

He first had the nightmare shortly after his dad's death. The dream always ended the same way: his crumpled body on the pavement outside his old apartment, waiting for the final blow from the unrecognizable attacker.

The night before he broke his finger, the nightmare gained two additions: First, he found himself moving toward a lighted building while running from his assailant, but he could never quite get there. Second there was that voice.

Time, Digger wondered, time for what? He glanced over at his VCR: 9:35 a.m. He sprang from his chair. The softball game was in forty-five minutes. Quickly he dressed in his uniform and surveyed the spotless cottage. It doesn't look half bad, he thought. Now maybe I can get some music written—soon as this game is over.

He went to the closet and dug out his totebag. He checked to make sure he had everything: two fielding gloves, aluminum bats, batting gloves, baseball shoes, sun glasses, and lots of gum. He slung the bag over his shoulder, took one last look around, and headed for the door.

The phone rang. He started to open the door and leave, but changed his mind. Who knows? It might be his mother. He didn't want to have to deal with another of her guilt trips.

"Hello?"

"Top a' the marnin' to ya, Patrick, me boy," Sean Green said. "I took a chance I wouldn't be wakin' ya, ya know."

"Yeah, Sean, what can I do for you?" Goosebumps suddenly covered his body. He broke out in a cold sweat. "I'm just on my way out the door," he added uncomfortably.

"Well, change yer plans, lad. What I've got to tell ya is a once-in-a-lifetime thing."

"What do you mean?" he asked, placing his totebag on the floor.

"Are ya sittin' down, me boy? This is liable to take your breath away, ya know. Ya might even start to think I'm playin' fast and loose with the truth."

"Please, just spit it out."

"Remember the tape ya sent me?"

"Of course."

"Well, today is yer lucky day, me boy! I just received a call from me friend up at Warner Studios; name's Philip Michaelson. He's an important director up there, don't ya know. I'd sent him a copy of yer tape. Well, he listened to it last night and thinks it's got possibilities." Green's voice rose. "He's thinkin', maybe even for a movie he has in production. So what do ya think about that?"

Digger's knees got weak. He fell into his couch, thoughts racing out of control. Was this really his lucky day or just another empty promise, masquerading as opportunity?

Neither man spoke.

"What's the matter, lad, cat got yer tongue?"

Digger cleared his throat. "So what happens next?"

"Ya get yourself up here, that's what. He wants to meet ya. He wants to hear ya play, son. Today."

"Today?"

"He wants to have ya on the set by six tonight. There's to be an audition, ya know. You and three others. What do ya think, lad; are ya up for it?"

Digger stood up and grabbed a pencil and paper from the top of the piano. His mind wouldn't function, but that was okay. He didn't want to think; he might go catatonic, betrayed by too much thought. His hands shook. "What's the address?"

"That's the good lad," purred Green's velvet voice. "I'll send a driver to meet ya at the train station in L.A. Can ya make the 11:37 from San Diego?"

Almost two hours, Digger thought. I'll call in sick, pack some clothes, reserve a motel near the lot, and throw my music in a valise. "That should be no problem," he said, trying to sound professional.

Green then gave Digger precise instructions on where to go and what to say. He left nothing to chance and made Digger read back what he'd dictated. Finally, the Irishman sounded like he was ready to end the conversation. "Now don't be put off by the format. Have ya ever auditioned before?"

"When I was in school, but not since."

"It'll come back to ya. You'll be playin' on stage in a theater. Michaelson and his staff will be there in the audience, but they probably won't say a word. They'll be putting ya on video, they will. The stage crew will tell ya where to go and when it's to be your turn. I'll be there, too, but we won't speak until it's all over. I don't want ya thinkin' 'bout anything else but yer music." He paused. "Are ya having any questions, lad?"

Digger couldn't think of anything .

"Well, if ya think of any, ya know me number. Remember, get there early, ya know. Best bib and tucker?" He hung up.

Digger chuckled out loud. He could never decide when an Irishman was asking a question. 'Best bib and tucker.' It was something his mother had always said, meaning "Get all dressed up to look the best you can." He guessed Green meant he should wear a tux, if he had one.

He took a long, deep breath. For some strange reason, the room felt warm now. The clean and salty smells of the ocean filled his nostrils. Outside, squawking sea gulls screamed and fought for a morning meal, while down below, four-foot breakers pounded the shore, reminding the world that they were still doing their job; minute by minute, hour by hour, year by year, century by century, from the beginning of time, old man sea was hard at work doing his job. He never stopped, never asked for sympathy or a day off. Just did his job.

Digger thought how nice it would be if he were the sea, then he'd know what he was supposed to be doing. He shook his head and went over to the piano. He sat down and gently began to play the opening to the transition piece. "Well, Taylor," he said out loud in his best Irish brogue, "are ya up for it, me boy?"

As usual, the train left late; most trains traveling the coastal route from San Diego to Los Angeles leave late. Digger knew that because he'd made this trip before, not for business but pleasure. The City of Angels had so many worthwhile cultural events that never came to San Diego and he wanted to see them all. With his ongoing money problems, it was one of the few extravagances he allowed himself. The last time was "The Phantom of the Opera" with the Broadway cast. He usually went alone. He just liked to absorb the beauty and joy of an opera or symphony or author's reading by himself.

Today, he easily found a double–seater on the ocean side of the train. Weekdays were great for finding good seats. This time, oddly, he thought it would have been perfect if he had some company.

Digger looked out the window at the pounding surf and white sandy beaches of Del Mar. As the train slowed to its stop, the sand reminded him of his meeting earlier that morning with Mary. Too bad about her impatience, he thought. She would have been fun to make the trip with. He always enjoyed her humor and insight. Actually, he would have been proud to have Mary hear his music when he finally got it sounding right. It just wasn't there, yet.

Settle down, Taylor. No sense getting bent out of joint. If you stay in the same old rut, you're just going to go up to L.A. and lay an egg. Like Green said, this is probably a once–in–a–lifetime shot. All the movie people care about is if you can produce. Green gave them the tape and they're interested, so you're on first base; that's the good news. Now you've got to get to second base, and your pinkie's the thing—well, not exactly. It's the phrases in the transition. That's the thing. You've got six hours to get yourself in a positive frame of mind. You've got to do something different. Something that will make that transition work.

Digger looked out the train window at the afternoon sun blazing down on the dark blue Pacific. It could just as easily have been the Atlantic. Funny, he thought, how oceans can look so much alike and yet carry such different emotional baggage. He remembered back ten years, when he'd been driving down from Chicago to the Florida Keys—twenty-five hours worth of thinking. Back then, he had been doing the same thing he was now: promising himself that he was going to do things differently.

His marriage to Ruth in Chicago had been a wrong decision from the start. He knew he didn't really love her with his whole heart—that kind of "till death do us part" love that he'd heard so much about in catechism. But while they were courting, and even during the first year of the marriage, it seemed they'd done the right thing.

They'd both given it their best shot, but, as it turned out, that wasn't enough. The fact was, neither of them had sufficient life experience to know what it took to make a relationship work. They both tried too hard and not hard enough. One of the main problems was they couldn't talk to each other; she was filled with fire-and-brimstone and he always had difficulty recognizing and expressing feelings. Instead of putting more energy into the relationship, he spent more time away from home, playing sports and performing in community theater.

Years later, after they were divorced, they sat down and talked. By that time, both had better perspectives on the relationship. Ruth said she could see how she had believed that marriage was the only legitimate way for an Irish Catholic girl to leave home. Digger explained that he'd been fulfilling society's script without knowing it: go to college, get a good job, fall in love, and get married.

Digger eventually forgave himself for that mistake. In fact, he learned from his Chicago career as a family counselor that most people aren't even aware of living out scripts that are not their own. But he told Ruth he'd always be sorry that, once he knew he needed to be out of the relationship, he did nothing about it. He kept those feelings and thoughts to himself. He played the ostrich, hoping that the problem would go away. By not saying anything to her, by staying in the relationship, he actually caused more damage.

It was no different than his reluctance to leave Chicago itself. A strong feeling of emptiness had haunted him for a number of years. Something called him, begged him to reach out, to be somewhere different, to do something different, to be different. But that would have meant leaving his wife, job, friends, sports, theater, and family. Who was he, if he didn't have these people and activities around him? So he stayed in a life of camouflaged emptiness, where no matter how busy he kept himself, that sinking feeling would eventually enter.

Digger firmly believed now that his hesitation had almost gotten him killed. God or someone had said, "Enough is enough," and sent him a message one hot Chicago weekend—a message he couldn't ignore.

The dinging bells of a railroad crossing and the long blast of the train's warning horn brought Digger back to the present. "Next stop San Juan Capistrano," bellowed a conductor. Digger looked around. A petite Hispanic woman with two children sat across the aisle from him.

The boy, who appeared to be about twelve, stood and looked up at the luggage compartment above Digger's head. "How are we going to get our stuff down?" he asked his mother in Spanish. "I can't reach it."

"Never mind," she answered in Spanish. "We'll get the conductor to help us. Just sit down. I don't want you to get hurt. The train is going too fast."

The boy reluctantly sat down, protesting the whole time. His little sister told him to stop being a show–off.

Digger watched and then turned to look out the window. He didn't want to seem like an eavesdropper just because he understood Spanish. Still, he wanted to help; they'd be waiting forever for another conductor to come by.

"Excuse me," he said finally, addressing the woman in English, "is there anything I can do to help?" He pointed at the luggage rack up above him. "Do you have something up there I could get down for you?"

The woman smiled.

"Yeah, man," said the boy in English. "We got all our stuff up there. She wants to have the conductor get it for us, but who knows when we'll see one of them again."

Digger smiled and nodded at the woman and her daughter. "Is that all right with you?" he asked in English.

The boy translated while the woman studied Digger. Then she nodded. *"Gracias, señor. Gracias."*

After he'd lifted all the baggage and paper bags down, he once again nodded to the woman, then turned to the boy. "Is that everything? Is there anything else I can do to help?"

"No. That's cool, man. We got it from here."

Digger went back to his seat.

The boy sat down next to him. "Thanks a lot, dude. Where you headed?"

"L.A."

"Gonna see the Dodgers play or something?"

"No. You like the Dodgers?"

"Yeah. They're my team, man. Mike Piazza's my main man, dude. Strongest man in Southern California. Awesome. Are you a Padre fan?" the boy asked.

"No, I'm actually a Cubs fan."

"But they lose all the time. Why d'ya root for them?"

Digger chuckled. "When I was growing up in Chicago, the only time I really got to see my Dad was when he let me come to his factory. Wrigley Field was only a block away. So I would sweep the floors in the morning and then go to the Cubs game in the afternoon." He thought for a second. "So began the honor or the curse, I still can't figure out which one, of being a Cubs Fan."

They both chuckled.

The boy continued, "They say that the people who follow the Cubs are die-hard fans. Is that true?" He sat back in the seat, clearly enjoying the conversation.

"I guess you could say that about me. When I was your age, I used to do some strange things to help the Cubs win.

"What do you mean?"

"I would bargain with God on baseball matters."

"You're kidding."

"Now don't tell me you never bargained with God before," Digger said, feigning a serious tone.

The boy hung his head. "Well, sometimes if I do something that I wasn't s'posed to. I'll tell God that I will go to church twice a week, if He gets me out of trouble."

"I did that, too," Digger smiled, "but about God and baseball, I would sit in a lawn chair under the maple tree in my front yard and listen to a Cubs game. I would keep the stats with my homemade scorebook. The Cubs would be battling to get out of last place, usually against the Phillies. Ernie Banks would be coming up in the bottom of the ninth—that's when my bargaining would begin. I didn't use the 'I'll go to church' bit. No, I bargained heavier chips than that. I would tell God that if he let Ernie hit a home run to win the game, I'd take a D in Geography. Depending on the game, I'd change the batters' names and my school subjects."

"Did it work?"

"Well I figured out that God must have been a White Sox fan." Digger looked the boy straight in the eyes. "Or maybe a Dodgers fan. Because the Cubs hardly ever won any of those games. What made it worse was trying to explain to my parents why I was getting so many D's on my report card!"

They both laughed out loud.

And as an adult with sixteen years' of Catholic education, Digger thought, I still don't have a clue about God and spirituality.

He changed the subject. "You play ball?"

"Yeah, man. Shortstop. All–star. That's me. That's what I want to be when I grow up—a baseball player."

"Jorge," barked his mother in Spanish. "Come over here and sit down. You're disturbing that man."

The boy raised his eyebrows, twisted his mouth, and sighed. "*Sì, Mama.*" He waved goodbye to Digger and took his seat beside his mother. The train was screeching to a stop.

The family thanked Digger profusely as they left. Jorge was the last to leave, arms filled with paper bags and small travel cases. "Thanks a lot, man," he said. "Whenever you watch or listen to the Dodgers, remember me, Jorge. Dodgers rule."

Digger smiled and held the door for the boy. After they were gone, Digger sat down, thinking back to when he was Jorge's age. He loved playing ball. He felt there was a certain poetry and grace about the game. People laughed at him when he tried to explain that, but with the advent of slow-motion playbacks, he figured everyone could finally see what he'd always felt.

There were other reasons that he loved to play ball: It wasn't the waiting for his dad to come home. It wasn't the complaining, yelling, or screaming from his mother. There was only him screaming, "I've got it!" as he camped under a fly ball. Only him running as fast as he could. Only him hitting, catching, yelling, sliding, and running till it was so dark he couldn't see the ball anymore. Then, and only then, would he stop running so he could walk home.

The compartment door just beyond Digger's seat swung open. "Next stop, Anaheim," bellowed a conductor, marching past. The train moved again.

Time to get your head together, Taylor.

Digger stared out the window of the train as it lumbered toward its next stop. This was the part he liked least. The scenery was nothing but freight yards and the bleak backroads, alleys, and abandoned buildings of southern L.A. County—something definitely worth missing.

He needed to figure out what he was going to do about the transition within his concerto—and what if his finger cramped up during the audition? Better not start thinking like that, Taylor. You better get your head in the game. He chuckled to himself—"head in the game"—baseball talk about playing the piano. Taylor, you're a mess. Still, that's the advice the boy would have given. Digger imagined how Jorge might have put it: "Come on, Taylor. Have a clue, dude. Get your head in the game, man; music rules."

His attention shifted back to the dreary scene outside. It reminded him of the south side of Chicago. His thoughts slowly drifted back to that horrible August weekend.

It was a typical August afternoon in Chicago—hot and muggy with both temperature and humidity in the nineties. In one week, his divorce would be final and two weeks later he'd be vacationing in Key West. Ever since he and his dad had visitied the islands off the southwestern tip of Florida, Digger wanted to scuba dive, to slip silently among the wonders of the coral reefs. Now his dream was coming true: He was standing on the sea wall getting ready for his last diving lesson, the final checkout before his certification. The heat was blasting off the cement rocks at the 55th St. jetty, but Digger pulled on a full wet suit. Lake Michigan would still be icy cold a few feet down. His diving instructor, an assistant, and two of Digger's friends were eager to jump into the cool lake. About fifteen diving tanks were lined up against the sea wall, full of compressed air that could either sustain life—or obliterate it if any one of the explosive tanks should crash against a rock. The dive master gave the last of his instructions, made sure everybody was "buddied-up," and with a final word of caution, they jumped into the refreshing water, one at a time. Once they were all in, they descended to the bottom, about twenty feet down. Visibility was only two to three feet, but Digger saw the diving instructor's buddy pick up a small, round-looking object. He swam closer to take a look.

The diver handed the object to Digger, who put it up to his mask to get a better look. He couldn't figure out what it was and shrugged his shoulders, then passed it back to the diver.

They all went through the checkout procedures: hand signals, taking their mask off and on, purging, breathing on the buddy system, and some compass diving. When their air pressure gauges read five hundred psi, they swam to the surface with their respective buddies.

Everybody brought out their sandwiches and soft drinks to celebrate. Digger was amazed at how hungry a little diving made him. Halfway through their meal, the small strange object was brought out for another look. The guys passed it around. When it got to Digger, he took another close look and then handed it to his buddy. The object was eventually thrown back to the diving instructor's friend. He caught it and went to put it back in his bag.

All Digger remembered was hearing a loud bang and seeing pieces of flesh and dark red fluid piercing the white phosphorous smoke that engulfed them. He thought the diving tanks were exploding and they were all going to be killed. He kept as low as he could and crawled along the cement. When the smoke had partly cleared, he saw the instructor putting a tourniquet on his friend's arm. Digger and his buddies picked up the remnants of the injured diver's hand.

The police surmised that someone must have finally tired of a World War II souvenir and tossed it in the lake—figuring it would be safe down there. But the British land mine detonator cost the diving instructor's buddy most of his hand.

The next night Digger and his two friends were still shaken up. They couldn't forget the gruesome scene of the day before. To let off some anxiety, they decided to go downtown and have a few beers. They started on Rush Street and worked their way through some jazz bars. After several hours and too many beers, they drove to a section of the city known as Old Town. It was a hot and muggy night and everybody and their sister was out on the streets—standing on the corners, talking, laughing, all having a good time. The traffic was so jammed that the pedestrians moved faster than the cars.

Digger and his friends were stuck behind a slow line of cars when a group of drunken guys left one of the pubs and walked over to the car. Digger, sitting in the back seat, felt shivers run up and down his spine. One of the drunks stuck his head in the back window. His breath stank of whiskey as he sang a couple of lines from an old Irish ballad: "Aren't ya tired of runn'n from the devil? Don't ya know, he's just like you and me." The man winked and gave Digger an evil smile as he turned and joined the rest of his cronies.

Oddly, Digger felt he had met this character before. He wasn't sure where or when, but he had seen him. No, he thought, not so much seen him as *felt* him.

"Hello," his buddies yelled at two attractive women walking the sidewalk by the car. As the car inched its way through traffic, the guys kept up a conversation with the women. It turned out they were all headed for the same bar; his buddies offered them a ride. One woman sat up front while the other sat next to Digger in the back.

They all laughed, giggled, and blurted out their life stories; then the girl in the front seat asked if they could pull down the next street. She said she needed to drop off a note at her girlfriend's apartment. They stopped for only a minute. When the young woman returned, she said it would be quicker if they took a shortcut through the next alley.

Digger flirted with the woman in the back seat as the car turned into the alley. A moment later, he realized that he was the only one talking. As he turned his head toward the front seat, he felt the cold steel of a gun pressed against his temple. Two things happened simultaneously: his heart felt as if it were going to pound through his chest and he consciously had to restrain his body's urge to eliminate.

After she took his buddies' wallets, the woman next to him reached into his front pocket and removed his money clip. No one had spoken a word. It was like a silent movie except for the sound of Digger's heart pounding in his brain. The woman in the front seat took the car keys as she told the three of them, "Have a nice night, boys." The two women walked away and dumped the car keys in a nearby trash bin.

The now sobered and stunned men sat in silence for what seemed like an eternity. Finally the driver rummaged through the glove compartment and came up with a spare key. As they drove home that night, Digger's emotions fluctuated from panic, to relief, to anger, to joy, to a feeling of being fairly stupid.

He went to work the next morning with a slight hangover. Before he could even tell his co-workers of his weekend from hell, he noticed three emergency status reports on his desk. They were all clients of his: John, a sixteen-year-old boy, was in the hospital for a drug overdose. Susan, a thirteen-year-old girl, was in the custody of Children and Family Services after her father had sexually abused her again. And Leon, a twelve-year-old, had set fire to his living room.

Digger spent the next twelve hours helping his clients and their families deal with their crises. That night, as he walked back into his office, he knew that whatever fears he had about leaving Chicago, family, and friends were totally gone. He didn't have an ounce of doubt as he walked over to the typewriter and typed out his resignation. He didn't know exactly what he was going to do, but he knew that whatever it was, it wasn't going to be in Chicago. Whoever or whatever had sent him a message. He got it. He didn't necessarily understand it—but he finally got it.

The compartment door slammed open and the noise of the speeding train blasted into Digger's ears. "Anaheim, next stop," bellowed the conductor. "Anaheim, next stop."

Digger sighed and looked at his watch. He shook his head and tried to clear the cobwebs from his mind. In therapy they called it "museum tripping"—going back and visiting events from one's past. Strange, but it seemed that his unconscious mind was hell-bent on visiting every little nook and cranny of his own private Louvre.

Chapter 4

"Who was he if he didn't have these people and activities around him?"

Less than four hours, Taylor, and you still don't have your game face on. You've really got to think about your finger and that transition piece. After all, thinking about those past crises is not going to help you now. You might as well have a backup plan just in case things fall apart during the audition.

Plan, he thought to himself. There's a word you haven't used in a while. Back in Florida, it seemed like that was the only word that came out of your mouth. Plan. Might even have helped. One thing you learned in Florida: it's not how you live out Plan A in life, but it's how you cope with Plan B.

"Anaheim," shouted a conductor. "Please watch your step going down the stairs."

The train lurched to a stop. The usual slow lines of passengers tried to get off. Outside, Digger saw people queuing up to get on. The train car was hot and muggy from the blazing sun and the open doors.

Digger yawned and nodded to three nuns who walked by his seat. Thirty more minutes or so, Taylor, and you're going to be getting into Sean Green's stretch limo and driving through L.A.'s early afternoon traffic to the audition of your life. Come on, Digger. Think about what you're going to do if you can't get it together. You don't want to make a damn fool of yourself. You've got to have a plan.

His eyelids were heavy. Digger tried to force his eyes back open, but he'd only had one hour's sleep this morning—and that was taken up by his recurring nightmare. *You've got to fight your way through this, Taylor. You can sleep all you want once the audition is over.*

In a few moments his eyes finally shut. Images of black and white criss-crossed under his eyelids. His mind raced back and forth between what people wanted him to do with his life and what he thought he wanted to do.

Life had never been that clear to Digger—never that black-and-white, though he believed his Catholic upbringing tried to make it that simple. Even on the big issues, such as God, life after death, and the soul. He had given up thinking about all of that a long time ago.

Digger's thoughts drifted back to being a young child who knew all the right answers to the Baltimore Catechism questions. But even knowing all that religion stuff still didn't fill his emptiness. In fact, it confused his mind, heart, and soul even more. Somehow the life he lived and the life he was supposed to live did not match. Religion had basically struck out, as far as he was concerned.

In fact, Digger still had some lingering anger about growing up Catholic. In his neighborhood, two sidewalks led to different schools. They were labeled by everyone in the community as "the Catholic sidewalk" and "the Public sidewalk"— "publics" were anyone who wasn't Catholic.

He was taught what most religions teach their constituents: that they are the Chosen Ones. Only Catholics would go to Heaven. As he got a little older, Digger realized that wasn't entirely true. There was a stipulation, at least in Catholicism, that if you died with a mortal sin on your soul, you would go to Hell. He quickly learned the reason for the confessional—to wipe out all those blemishes.

A couple of years after Jonathan came into the age of reason, the ramifications of some of the teachings sunk into his little head: his father was a Lutheran and would not be allowed into Heaven. He was told that the best his father could hope for was to get into Purgatory. Kind of like where he's been his whole life, Digger thought to himself. This concept didn't sit well with him. Although he hardly saw his father, he still believed that his dad was the greatest. No nun could tell him any different. He never expressed that little animosity inside of him, but within his head he made the call—Strike 1.

Nuns were strong disciplinarians. They could be tough, mean, and controlling. Digger believed they were the hand of God sent to keep every child in line.

When he was about to graduate from grammar school, raging hormones had already begun to move through his body. One day this bodily process became the subject of discussion. Any questions on morality in the class, as in most cases, revolved around "If I do ... is that a sin?" A boy in the back of the class asked about erections and their relationship to sin. Digger couldn't believe anyone would ask that question! He'd been thinking about it for several months, but he never dared ask it.

The sister confidently answered, "It is a venial sin."

The boy chimed in, "Even if you're not thinking about it and it just happens?"

Without missing a beat, the sister retorted, "Of course."

Digger felt instantly guilty—that was one of the things he learned very well—but he was also confused. He could understand it being a sin if he was thinking "dirty" thoughts about one of the girls in his class. He felt responsible for his own thoughts. But sometimes he'd get aroused out of nowhere; he wasn't thinking about anything in particular, it would just happen.

His mind started to keep count for the confessional: let's see, about twelve times a day; multiply that by seven days a week, then four weeks a month. He figured out that he must be in serious trouble. He couldn't even imagine how much the penalty would be if you touched it! Under his breath, but loud enough for the sister to hear, Digger's classmate whispered, "Bullshit."

In eight years, nobody had said those words within a mile of school. The sister promptly came over and slapped the boy's face hard enough to make an imprint. The boy was stunned. The class was stunned. Digger felt the blow as if the nun had hit him. He'd had the exact same thought but would never express it. The discussion period was officially over—Strike 2.

Digger thought back through all the times he'd been hit on the knuckles for his supposedly poor piano-playing technique. But he dismissed all those whacks as swings and foul balls.

The final pitch came when he went to confession during his sophomore year of high school. He opened the door to the darkened box and knelt. As he recited "Bless me, father, for I have sinned; it has been ten months since my last confession," the priest stopped Digger right then and there. The darkened face behind the veil proceeded to give him a lecture about the excessive length of time between confessions. Digger's first reaction was confusion: he'd been proud of himself for even going to confession. But then he got angry. He wanted to scream at the priest about all those things he felt were wrong with religion: about his dad not being able to go to Heaven; about the nuns' unrealistic expectations of growing young men; about music being taught by form and not feeling; about teaching people rules, limits, and fear instead of love, essence, and acceptance.

He wanted to say all those things—but he didn't. He slowly got up from his knees as the priest continued his lecture and walked out, never to return—at least in mind and heart. Strike 3.

"Los Angeles main station," bellowed the voice. "Last stop. Los Angeles, last stop."

Digger bolted up in his seat and blinked open his eyes. The roar of a speeding train filled the compartment. The other passengers were ready to get off. The conductor was halfway down the aisle. "Next stop Los Angeles," he bellowed again.

Digger rubbed his eyes as he stood up, grabbing his garment bag from the compartment above. Through Digger's study of philosophy, which began in college, he had tried to discover the heart of what he believed religions might be seeking, what he might be seeking. But there were never enough words, ideas, or concepts to fill his void.

Digger shook his head and tried to focus back on the present. Come on, Taylor. You're almost there and you still haven't figured out what Plan B is. Thinking about the core of your emptiness is not going to get you anywhere. Surely, you don't expect to win an audition without a backup strategy. It isn't as if you had two or three more auditions waiting for you. You need to come up with a way to gracefully bridge from one movement to the other without crashing and burning; you've got to go all out, but still have an escape plan.

The noise broke his concentration. As the train braked, the sounds of rumbling steel against steel was deafening; behind him, a baby began to cry.

Great, he thought. I guess I'll have to figure out Plan B when I'm in the peace and quiet of that stretch limo Sean Green is sending. Thank God for Sean Green.

The train slowed to a stop.

I hope old Sean Green wasn't kidding; I wouldn't want to have to find Warner Studios by myself. That would be a real nightmare.

With a suit bag slung over his shoulder and a valise in the other hand, Digger left the comfort of the train and walked down the long platform toward the heart of the station. He studied the faces of the people greeting passengers. He'd been told to look for someone with a large printed sign with his name on it. As he joined the crowd walking down the long, wide, echoing corridors, Digger's anxiety rose.

He looked up at a wall clock. *Just a little over three hours till the audition, and I'm still messing around trying to get there—don't even know what I'm going to do when I do get there. This is stupid. I shouldn't have come. I'm not ready for the big leagues. No one's going to let me score a movie. I'm nobody. There are thousands of experienced composers and songwriters with more credentials than I'll ever have. Why'd I let Green talk me into this?*

"Mister Taylor?" Digger heard a female voice call; it was somewhere behind him. "Mister Jonathan Taylor, if you can hear me, please raise your hand," said the rising sing–song voice.

Digger did as he'd been asked.

"Oh, there you are," smiled a redhead, materializing from the throng. "Well, I'm Monica," she said, extending her white–gloved hand. "Mister Green sent me to make sure you got to Warner Studios in plenty of time. Let me take those," she said, reaching for Digger's suit bag and valise.

"Thank you," he said as he handed it to her. "Lead the way."

She weaved her way through the crowded station toward a long, white stretch Mercedes, parked in a loading zone. By now, she was way ahead of him and Digger was forced to wait while several taxis, loaded with new passengers, shot from their parking spaces and sped by. As he began to cross the driveway, a familiar flash of panic swept through him:

How would I get out of the way of an oncoming vehicle? I have to be careful and keep a watchful eye. Can't just hope things are going to turn out all right.

Digger always had those thoughts when he crossed streets in heavy traffic. A heightened sense of awareness and caution would flash through him. The feeling had always puzzled him: he'd never been hit by a car and he didn't know anyone who had—he had no reason to be afraid.

He frowned as he jogged up to the parked white limo. Whenever he exercised his legs, it felt good; maybe jogging would help put him in the right frame of mind. That's what he should do once he got to Warner Studios: find a place to jog, if there was time.

Monica held open the rear door to the limo. "You all right, Mister Taylor?"

Digger nodded and slid onto the new tan leather upholstery covering the back seat. Monica got in the driver's side, started the engine, and electronically closed the one–way glass window just behind her seat. A phone underneath his armrest buzzed.

Digger picked it up, not quite sure what to expect. "Hello?"

"You want to stop anywhere?" Monica purred.

"No, thank you," he replied, relaxing a bit. "Just take me to Warner Studios as fast as you can without getting a ticket. I'd like to beat the traffic if we can." He paused. "Oh yes. I'm going to try and take a little nap so I'd appreciate it if you made sure I wasn't disturbed."

"Shhure," she sing–songed.

Digger switched the phone to the "off" position before replacing it. Now he could do some serious meditating. When his finger was broken he couldn't play softball or the piano, so he'd had plenty of time to practice his meditation. It was something he'd never done until he came to California—but he usually put it off until he was really stressed out. Maybe someday he'd learn to meditate before the stress became unbearable.

Digger slid off his tennies and eased back into a comfortable position in the back seat. His shoulders felt like they were attached to his ears. He closed his eyes and concentrated on his breathing. That was the ticket: focus on the breathing—nothing else mattered. In a few moments his breathing slowed. His body relaxed more with every breath.

As soon as he'd completely relaxed, a heaviness came over him—and a feeling that something was wrong. He hadn't felt anything so strong since Florida. It reminded him of his premonitions in Key West, when the negative energy had become so intense—especially toward the end. He'd known the end was coming for some time, but he didn't have the guts to level with Judy—or himself.

Digger was twenty–seven when he left Chicago for Key West. It had been two weeks since his nearly-fatal weekend. He needed time to figure out his life. He thought the trip to Florida would be a nice little vacation—for a month or so. Then he'd go to San Diego to get on with his life. Digger had always felt a pull to that city, even though he'd never been there. He was sure, almost sure, that that was where he was supposed to be.

But his vacation in the Keys lasted almost six years. When he first arrived, he went fishing on the same boat he and his dad had chartered several years before. The captain mentioned that he needed a new mate to crew the 32-foot fishing vessel, and Digger, in a rare fit of spontaneity, asked for the job. He got it. At least it was different from his old job as a social worker, he reasoned. The change felt good, too. As he got up each morning to the smell of fresh salt–water breezes and the sound of the ocean lapping up onto the shore, he felt invigorated.

Then he met Judy. She was there on the Gulf Oil docks everyday when his boat refueled. He'd never known an "Aussie" before and Digger was enchanted by her speech. With words alone it was almost as if she made music that weaved a spell around him. She was an attractive woman from head to toe, but a few years older than he. Although tall—about five-foot-seven—she moved like a cat. Judy introduced him to the finer culinary tastes: she was not only an excellent chef—she made an ordinary meal a sensuous event.

Thinking back now, he realized that sensual quality must have influenced his better judgment. He wound up opening a restaurant with Judy. At the time it just seemed like it was meant to be. That's what his intuition said. They decided he should move into her place when they hatched the plan.

But as soon as they opened The Kangaroo's Pouch on a converted houseboat—"The Best Seafood From Down Under"—all the signs changed. It was as if someone in charge of the galaxy had turned on this giant energy switch labeled "Challenge." Toward the end, the whole ordeal in Florida was a nightmare. His relationship with Judy went through several cycles: on, off, hot, cold, and many rinses. He'd forgotten the old adage: "Never go into business with your friend or lover."

Just as in Chicago, Digger knew he should have exited the whole ordeal long before the end was forced on him. His feeling of emptiness grew strongest during the last year. But as usual, though, he stayed on. He couldn't leave. That would have meant leaving his business, friends, and sports. Who was he if he didn't have these people and activities around him?

He remembered one particularly painful day in Key West. He'd slept on the couch and left the apartment at the crack of dawn. Judy had lost interest in sex about three years back. At that time, he'd rationalized that things would work themselves out as soon they both got used to the new routine. He was wrong. Not only did she not want to make love, sometimes he'd wake up in the middle of the night and she'd be sound asleep, kicking at him with her feet. That's how he ended up on the couch the night before.

It was early morning when he showed up at The Kangaroo's Pouch, architect's plan in hand. Judy was already there. As usual, she was in the kitchen cleaning. He tried to explain a new idea he had for improving the business. He'd asked a friend to sketch out a floor plan with some new equipment.

She didn't say a word—she just washed and shook her head no.

"Can't you see?" Digger pleaded. "The only way we can make it here is to turn our tables over two or three times each mealtime," he said, pacing the first floor of the double–decker houseboat. In one hand, he carried the rolled up floor plan, tape measure in the other. "This'll work, honey. Won't you even look at it?"

"Not likely, mate," she said, pale–faced, tight–lipped, and looking into the dirty oven. "I know your game: more equipment, faster turnover, warming tables, food without nutritional value, take the money and run, and screw the blinking customer."

"Screw the customer? What do think we're doing now? Hell, we're lucky if we can feed them in a frigging hour!"

"You bastard!" she screamed, throwing a bristle brush at him.

He ducked and the brush slid across the floor.

Judy broke into tears. "If you think you can do it better, then you get in here and try cooking any faster."

He went over and picked up the brush, sat down at one of the tables, and sighed.

"This plan isn't a commentary on your cooking, Judy," he said finally, in a gentle voice. "We both know no one could do better. But because of our inexperience, we designed this place to fail. Good food is one thing, but this is a business. The point is to make a profit, and we've been losing our ass. Hell—our insurance policy on the boat was canceled yesterday because we had to pay our suppliers!"

"What about 'The Best Seafood From Down Under'? Doesn't that mean anything? How can it be the best if it's coming straight off some bloody–arse Yank steam table?"

"We can still serve the best seafood and make money; it just requires a plan." He picked up the drawing. "The guys down at the restaurant supply store will even barter some equipment for free meals. Won't you just look at it?"

She went back to scrubbing and didn't answer.

Digger seethed. The now-familiar pain in his stomach quickly intensified. He picked up his tape measure and slammed the door behind him.

Judy spun around. "And good riddance to smelly rubbish, mate! I hope all hell freezes over before I see your two–sided Yank face again!"

Digger moved out that day. A few days later, Judy got word to him that if he wanted to advertise the restaurant for sale, that'd be fine with her. He should have known better.

Within twenty-four hours of placing the ad, a qualified buyer for the business came forward and made a good offer. When Digger called Judy to tell her about it, he was beside himself with excitement. Maybe things were going to turn out well after all. Maybe all this heartache and hard work was going to finally bear fruit. The phone rang only twice.

"Are you there?" she said in her flip Aussie twang.

"It's me, Judy," he said.

"Oh ... hello, mate. What's up?"

"We've got a buyer, Judy. Can you believe it? We've got an honest–to–God buyer who's ready with cash."

"How much?"

"Seventy–five. It's cash, though, and he's ready to settle tomorrow or whenever we say."

Silence.

"That's not what we agreed," she said coldly. "We agreed to sell for one hundred thousand dollars."

"I know, Judy, but it's cash. Usually these things get dragged out for years and years and you have to sue for your money and it's a mess. This is cash. No if's, and's, or but's."

She cleared her throat. "Now you listen to me, Mr. Taylor," she said, her voice rising. "I'm sick and tired of your bloody Yank bullshit. I said one hundred thousand and that's what I meant. Not one dollar less. Do I make myself clear, mate?" She was yelling by now.

Digger's tempered boiled. "Quite clear that you had no intention of selling." He slammed down the phone.

After that, the ominous feeling really started rearing its ugly head. He'd come home at night, bone tired after working all day on the boat. Soon as he'd showered and eaten, a strong negative energy would overtake him until he went down to Garrison Bight and made sure The Kangaroo's Pouch was okay.

There he'd be, hidden in the shadows. He tried to make sure no one saw him but he had to be certain everything at the restaurant was in good order. He checked the moorings and listened for the sounds of any dissatisfied customers as they sat at their tables. From the sounds he heard, things seemed to be going well. Still, Digger's sense that something was wrong wouldn't abate; instead it got worse.

A few nights later, after the restaurant closed for the day, he put on his scuba gear and slipped unnoticed into the warm Gulf sea water. With a borrowed underwater lamp, he checked the underside of the houseboat. While he searched for any defects, he thought he saw the shadow of a man standing on the wooden pier.

Everything looked in good order. Of course, there were a few barnacles and some algae, but nothing to worry about—nothing unusual or dangerous to the safety of the boat.

As he pulled himself up onto the pier, he looked for the shadowy figure but didn't see anyone. He took off his fins and mask. A vaguely familiar tune wafted though the warm night air. It was difficult to hear anything clearly as his ears were still clogged with water, but it sounded like a familiar Irish ballad.

Digger went back to his apartment but it was a long time before he could go to sleep. A storm was building and the rustling palm fronds seemed to be mimicking the words of that ballad: "Aren't ya tired of runn'n from the devil? Don't ya know, he's just like you and me."

When he awoke, the feeling was worse. It seemed like he had just fallen asleep. All he could hear was the rain pounding against the windows and roof and outside walls of his newly-rented condo. The noise was so loud and incessant, it reminded him of hail storms in Chicago. Only now, the wind howled and swirled like an angry, cornered beast trying to escape capture—charging wildly in one direction, then another and another. It wouldn't let up. Its charges became more furious and powerful with each new roar. Digger's condo creaked and groaned, while sheets of rain pelted the building.

The Kangaroo's Pouch!

Digger bolted up and looked outside onto Atlantic Boulevard. Most of the street lights still worked. Between gusts, he could see the shadow of palm trees that bent and swayed like oversized stalks of corn. Some had already snapped and fallen to the ground. Broken branches and lawn chairs and debris littered the streets and yards. This was the worst night squall he'd seen in Key West. He guessed the winds to be 50 or 60 m.p.h.

He knew it was dangerous, but he had to get to the restaurant. He couldn't just stay inside and do nothing while everything he and Judy had slaved night and day for was in danger. This must have been what his negative feelings were all about. He had to go down there. Digger threw on some old clothes and a rain parka. He wasn't sure if his VW Bug would start in this downpour. After a few tries, the engine finally turned over.

Slowly, Digger inched his way toward Garrison Bight. The streets were awash with cascading waters, palm leaves, branches, newspapers, spilled garbage cans, and frogs. The storm was sweeping away everything in its path. The ocean would quickly claim all this debris. He prayed there wouldn't be any high water accumulations; as long as the runoff remained no higher than a foot or so, he'd be all right. A wiseguy driver with a jacked-up truck body flew by and buried him with a wave of water. But the VW kept plugging along. Actually, despite the wind and flooded streets, Digger felt cleansed in some strange way by the rain.

Eventually, Digger and the VW made it to the parking lot next to the wind–swept bight. He drove as close as he could to the slips and aimed his high beams onto the bobbing and bouncing boats. It was too dark; he couldn't see The Kangaroo's Pouch. He grabbed a flashlight and ran down the swaying wooden walkway, shining the light through the blowing rain where his houseboat ought to be. The restaurant just had to be there, he told himself. It'd come through worse storms than this. His eyes must be playing tricks on him in this wind.

They weren't. It wasn't there. He found nothing but floating food and garbage, tables, chairs, and a sign bobbing in the water: "The Best Seafood From Down Under." Broken tie–lines drifted uselessly in the surging, muddy waters. The Kangaroo's Pouch had served its last meal.

He suddenly felt the urge to vomit: the canceled insurance policy; the sale that never happened; all that work; all those hours of sleep denied; all the time he and Judy never spent together just relaxing and enjoying each other like they had when they first met; all the time not spent doing things he wanted to do, like playing the piano and composing new music; all the sweat–labor spent fixing and building and cleaning and planning; all the fights and arguments and hostility; all those thousands and thousands of hours of precious time; all the hard–earned money both of them had poured into it ... gone ... gone forever. And for what?

Digger's skin grew clammy as his stomach cramped. In one swift involuntary movement, all that had been within him was violently projected into the white-capped water.

"Mister Taylor?"

Digger felt his shoulder being tugged.

"Mister Taylor, we're here."

He jumped up in his seat. The sun was shining brightly and he was in the back seat of the Mercedes limo. Monica was leaning over him.

"Safe and sound," she smiled, batting her baby browns. "Warner Studios sound stage number twenty-four, just like Mister Green said."

Chapter 5

"Your knowing is about to exceed your dreams."

"**M**y name is Taylor," Digger said to the regal–looking man behind the high, metal security stand. Dressed in a gray uniform with gold trim, the man's name tag read: Al White. Directly behind him was an iron stairway and railing that went up one story to a steel door. Beside it, the words "Sound Studio 24" were painted in large brown letters over a white masonry wall.

"I'm supposed to be here," Digger continued, "for a six o'clock audition with Mr. Michaelson."

The tall guard with well–cut silver hair and manicured nails pushed a walkie–talkie to one side and checked a list of names on his clipboard. "Ah, yes, Mr. Taylor," said White. "You're on my list. But you're a little early."

"I'm sorry," said Digger, as he put down his valise and adjusted his grip on the suit bag. "I just took the train up from San Diego and came straight here. Is there someplace I can wait if you can't let me in now?"

White nodded. "I guess it's all right. Come on, I'll show you to your dressing room." The security officer holstered the walkie–talkie and led the way up the stairs.

Digger followed, looking out across the Warner lot as he climbed the steps. On one side of the two-story studio was a street set where "Serpico" or "West Side Story" could have been made. On the other side was an outdoor Western set where scenes from "High Noon" or "Pale

Rider" might have been shot. In the distance he saw long, two and three–story buildings made of masonry and stucco; short, squat buildings made of glass and steel; and ugly, brick buildings that looked as if they'd had several additions. Connecting the buildings were blacktop streets, parking lots, and sidewalks. People drove cars or rode bikes or walked about as if they were on the grounds of any other large corporation. They seemed to regard movie–making as pretty routine stuff.

For Digger, there was nothing routine about being on the Warner lot. His heart raced and he could barely breathe. The persistent and growing sense that someone sinister was stalking him wouldn't go away, yet his mind whirled with the excitement of the moment. He was going to perform his own music; someone actually wanted to hear what he had written.

At the top of the stairs, the guard opened the door and said, "Just follow me." They walked down a long corridor which ended with a dozen steps that led to another closed door. The two men mounted the stairs. Inside was a plush theater, filled with sloped rows of extra–wide viewing seats, thick carpeting, and expensive lighting. Up high, along the back wall, Digger saw a projection and lighting booth with the normal cutouts and spotlights aimed at the low stage in front. In the middle of the stage stood a black Steinway and a Toshiba synthesizer, side–by–side before a red curtain.

"That's where you'll be performing," said the guard, pointing to the stage while they walked along the rear of the theater. "The dressing rooms are this way." He pointed to a door along the far wall near the back of the room.

Digger followed. "How are the acoustics in here?" he asked, as he readjusted his suit bag.

"The best," said the guard, "but you don't have to worry. They won't go too much on how you do here tonight; they'll be recording you on voice and video. Later, after it's all over, Mr. Michaelson and his staff will come back and listen to how you and the others did for hours."

Digger felt his throat getting dry. Listen for hours?

The guard opened the door to the dressing rooms and headed down another long, carpeted corridor. They passed a few doors. "Your dressing room is just ahead. Your competitors will be occupying some of these other ones, but I'm going to give you the best one since you got here first and came the furthest. It's soundproof and has its own piano and shower; even has a well–stocked refrigerator and liquor cabinet."

"Good grief," said Digger. "Thank you very much. I hope this isn't going to get you into any kind of trouble."

"Nah," said the guard. "No big deal—happens every day. Mr. Michaelson does this all the time. Almost every key position or acting part is filled by a staged audition. Nobody else I know of does it that way, but it's hard to knock success. Those young pups running the front office at least have the good sense to leave him be."

White stopped and pointed. "See that door at the end of the hallway? That's the entrance to the stage you'll go through when it's your turn."

Digger nodded.

White opened a door they'd been standing beside. "And this is your dressing room."

The visitor from San Diego stepped inside. The smell of fresh carpeting and drapes and paint filled his senses. The walls were paneled with stained ash except where the dressing table was with its tall mirrors. Beside it were closets and a large bath. Along the adjacent wall was a shiny black baby grand piano. Plush couches and club chairs were grouped with hardwood coffee tables for intimate conversation. Fresh flowers and plants were strategically placed. Opposite the dressing table, a well–stocked wet bar was topped by a brimming bowl of ripe fruit.

Digger whistled. "Man, you weren't kidding," he said as he walked around and shook his head. He peeked in the bathroom and opened the closet doors. "Look at this place. It's like no dressing room I've ever seen."

"So you've been in the movies before, Mr. Taylor?"

"No, just some amateur theater in Florida and Chicago. I've never seen anything like this, though. Most dressing rooms I've seen are smaller than a postage stamp." He reached in his pocket. "I really appreciate this, Mr. White. This is great."

The silver–haired guard held up his hand. "No thanks. I can't accept money. Thanks for your gracious words, though. Most of the people who come in here seem to take all this for granted. If you feel welcome, that's thanks enough for me."

"Well I do. I can't thank you enough."

White grinned, then left Digger on his own.

Digger hung up his suit bag and then took a quick shower. He slipped on some dress shorts and a tennis shirt; it was too early yet to put on his tux.

Time to work on the music, Taylor. That's why you're here, remember? You can't postpone the moment of truth forever. There's got to be a way to bridge from the first to the second movement with or without your friend, the pinkie.

He sat down at the piano and thought of all the years it had taken him to get back into playing and composing again. He'd shut out his music after the vacation with his dad in Key West.

When his father died a few months later, Digger's guilt washed the notes from his head and the music from his heart. Three years ago, he started to compose this "concerto that needed to be heard."

Now he sighed and tried to focus on the brighter side. "Look where I am now," he said to the empty room.

He stared down at the eighty-eight keys. Why not start with the second movement this time? As his fingers glided over the keys, his thoughts drifted back to the last Thanksgiving holiday with his mother in south Chicago.

"Digger's working on a new symphony," she'd announced to her friends. "You should hear it, ladies," she said, sitting down and sipping her pink Chablis. "It sounds like Bach or something."

He'd blushed a deep red. He didn't want to embarrass her in front of her friends, but he was tired of his mother's exaggerations about his piano playing.

"Oh, we'd love to hear your symphony," said one of the women. "We don't care if it's finished or not. Just play a part of it."

He smiled graciously. "That's kind of you," he said, "but I'm afraid I can't. The work is incomplete."

"Oh–h–h–h, what a shame," said his mother, wiping at her eyes. "Probably the only time I'll ever get a chance to hear my own son play his symphony for me in person."

Digger took another deep breath. "Mother, if you're going to try and trick me into into playing, you might as well call it by its correct name. It's a piano concerto, not a symphony."

"Symphony, concerto—they're all the same. What's the big deal? I don't give a damn about what it's called, I only want to hear you play it."

Holding his breath, he rose and slowly crossed to the piano. No one said a word. He sat down and began to play. By some powerful act of will, he was able to put the anger he felt for his mother at that moment out of his mind and concentrate on his playing. It was then that it came to him: begin the second movement *mezzo forte* and *staccato*, build to *forte* and *ritardando*, and end it *legato* and *adagio*. He rewrote the piece as he played, and the new way made all the difference. The whole concerto took on new life.

The women clapped and cheered. "Bravo!" they exclaimed, "Bravo! Encore!"

Digger's mother almost spilled her Chablis as she hurried over to kiss his cheek. "That was wonderful, Jonathan," she purred, "just wonderful." She kissed him again. "You make me so proud."

Now sitting in the dressing room on the Warner lot, Digger's fingers flew over the keys. He was barely conscious of where he was. All he could see was his mother's face; all he could hear were her words, "You make me so proud."

A loud knock on the door interrupted his reverie.

Startled, Digger stopped playing and sat still. He shook his head and tried to get his bearings. "Who is it?"

"Message for Mr. Taylor."

Digger opened the door. A stage hand gave him a note. He ripped open the hand–written envelope. Inside, the message read:

Dear Mr. Taylor:

Thank you for coming on such short notice. I appreciate that what I'm putting you through (even by Hollywood standards) is both highly unusual and unnerving, to say the least. Nevertheless, please indulge me; experience shows that my unorthodox selection process produces positive results.

Thanks and good luck,
Philip Michaelson

P.S. My staff drew straws for all participants; you drew last position. Your audition will take place at approximately 7:30. I'll send someone to warn you 15 minutes before.

Digger looked at his watch: 5:45. Less than two hours until his audition and he still didn't have a bridge between the first and second movements. He was probably going to have to go with the safe and mundane transition he'd played this morning in his cottage.

Every muscle in his body was tense. He suddenly felt overwhelmed by exhaustion. It was like what he imagined a marathon runner felt when they hit "the wall." My God, I haven't had any real sleep all day; it's been nothing but catnaps. He removed his tennis shoes, found a blanket in the closet, and stretched out on the couch.

A nap will do me good—refresh my energy and
concentration, he thought. This feeling of doom has really
drained me, and it seems to be getting worse. I need sleep.
Wasn't it Vince Lombardi who said fatigue makes
cowards of us all? That's probably why I feel like
everything in my life is about to go down the drain. I need
to relax for a little while—just a couple of minutes—then
I'll be ready to face anything.

Digger took a deep breath and closed his eyes. He went
through his well-rehearsed muscle relaxation technique,
starting with his feet and slowly moving to his head. When
he felt all his muscles relax, he focused solely on his
breathing.

Meditation. That's what you should do: meditate. Just
concentrate on your breathing. Inhaaale … Exhaaale … He
continued to focus on his breath; strangely, it was easier
than usual. He was going much deeper than he'd ever gone
before. Already he was feeling lighter and lighter, falling
through dark space—becoming smaller and smaller until all
he was conscious of was his breathing.

Out of nowhere a feeling of panic coursed through his
veins. The nightmare started. His limp body was thrown
around his old apartment. Again Digger felt the
excruciating pain as he flew through the window and hit
the pavement. He gasped for air. His skin felt as if it was
being pricked by needles as wind and rain pounded his
body. Digger struggled to his feet and ran down the barren
sidewalk for what seemed like an eternity. His attacker
followed relentlessly. Digger spotted a park and a building
in the distance, set way back from the street. He noticed
there was a light on. Maybe there were people inside who
could help him.

Now he felt as if he were running as fast as the wind,
crossing the street toward the park. But his pursuer was
still close behind.

Suddenly the rain stopped. He was running in the park
and it wasn't nighttime anymore. The sun was shining and
the sky was clear and light blue. In fact, it was a beautiful

day. The park was huge and green and lush, displaying a stunning array of forms and hues. It reminded him of an impressionist painting: there were flowers, plants, foliage, and birds of all sizes, shapes, and colors. A small stream fed into an iridescent lake; its calm waters silhouetted a peaceful sky.

Digger looked over his shoulder; his pursuer had gained some ground and seemed bigger in the daylight. Dressed in black, he appeared powerful and athletic. His face was hidden by long, dirty–blond hair. Digger kept running. Where's that building I saw the lights coming from?

As he rounded a clump of bushes and trees, Digger spotted the two–story stucco building with the lighted sign out front. It read: "The Celestial Bar," and underneath in smaller letters, "food and spirits." The light from the sign created a soft, inviting glow that drew him closer. A smoked glass façade covered the front of the building, allowing him to see the outlines of people milling about inside. Finally help, he thought. He hadn't seen anyone else in the park except his attacker. He looked up at the sign again. He had the strange sensation he'd been here before—maybe more than once.

As Digger touched the bronze door handle, an overwhelming panic seized him. He had no idea what was inside, but he intuitively felt that once he entered the bar, his life would never be the same.

He withdrew his hand and put it in his pocket. Chills ran through his body. But these chills were different; they were not only on his skin but were moving within him. He couldn't figure out which was worse—fear of the unknown inside the bar, or fear of more blows from his attacker.

He remembered how many times indecision had plagued his life: deciding whether to express his feelings or hold them inside; wavering on whether to quit his job in Chicago or stay; arguing with himself about leaving Ruth and Judy or sticking it out; saying something, anything to his dad or ...

He looked toward the park and saw the assailant was speeding toward him. He was tired of the pain. He looked at the bar's entrance. It was time for something different. He opened the door to The Celestial Bar.

At first it seemed dark inside. Digger took a minute to let his eyes adjust to the unusual lighting. He blinked and tried to focus on his surroundings. The first thing he noticed was that he felt different: his anxiety and fear were gone. And the guy chasing him didn't seem to be such a threat for the moment.

After his eyes adjusted, the light actually seemed brighter than outside, but softer—less harsh. Objects appeared translucent. He could see people eating and drinking. It was a richly appointed bar.

Out of nowhere, a man with dark skin and shiny black hair that hung below his shoulders appeared before Digger. He was wearing jeans and a flannel shirt. Digger's attention was drawn to his large grin, which exposed the man's sparkling, even teeth. His deep brown eyes were filled with kindness and laughter, his hands were large and weathered. Digger wondered if he was a Native American.

"Shoshone," said the man matter-of-factly.

Digger's jaw dropped and the man roared with laughter. "How did you know what I was thinking?" asked Digger.

The people in the bar turned and looked at the man laughing.

"Jonathan, it is about time," said the tall, dark man as he put his arms around Digger and gave him a bear hug—firm, but not too tight. Then he let go, giving the new arrival a broad smile. "It is so good to see you," he said as if welcoming an old friend.

Jonathan scowled. "Do you know me?"

The man nodded, and his smile turned to wry amusement. "Yes, I know you. My name is Ahmay. Come, let me show you to a seat. We have much to discuss."

As soon as Ahmay said his name, Jonathan felt as though they'd met before. The stranger led the way and Jonathan followed, looking around.

The room was fairly large—big enough to seat at least two hundred. The walls were decorated with a form of art that Jonathan had never seen before—it reminded him of holographics and impressionism combined into one medium. Some of the walls were decorated with small disk–like shields which concealed indirect lighting. Fireplaces lined one of the walls. A grand piano made of dark oak was positioned in the far corner. A few tables and chairs filled the center of the room, but mostly the customers sat in high-backed booths with plush, form–fitting seats. Each booth featured a shiny new hardwood table. Light from the unusual indirect fixtures reflected in the smooth–polished mahogany.

The bar itself was made of dark, rich mahogany to match the tables and booths. It was about a hundred feet long, and its elegantly hand–carved lines dominated the room. Behind the bar, equally beautiful wall units and mirrored sections set off the dark wooden bar. Well–placed flora and fauna added to the stunning effect.

As Ahmay slid into the booth opposite Jonathan, the expression on the Native American's face changed. He bent forward with a serious look in his eye. "What I should have said is that it is so good to see you in this way."

"What are you talking about?"

The Native American studied his guest. "Some of your knowingness will begin to come back to you shortly, but you are still in transition shock."

Jonathan shook his head. "Excuse me, Mr. Ahmay, but I have no idea what you're talking about. Transition shock? Are you sure I'm the right guy? This isn't a case of mistaken identity or something, is it? I have problems enough without being taken to be someone I'm not."

Ahmay smiled. "Most people do not make this journey before their time is up. For many years you have been Bear, but now, you have come back to the cave. Like the lost cub, you have decided to come home before embarking on a new path."

Jonathan started to leave the booth. "I'm sorry. I don't know who you are or what you're talking about. Everything you say sounds like gibberish. I don't mean to be rude, Mr. Ahmay, but I've got to go. I'm in deep trouble."

Ahmay's smile grew as he pushed the long hair out of his eyes. "I am sorry," he said, touching Jonathan's arm. "I am moving too fast for you. You will feel better after some nourishment. Think of me as your personal maitre' d."

"For what?"

"Your stay here at The Celestial Bar. My job is to provide information and comfort. I will be by your side through the whole experience—almost like a guide. While you are here, you will be known as Jonathan. But before we get into details, would you like to order? Our menu is without parallel."

Jonathan was dumbstruck by the avalanche of thoughts tumbling through his mind. Food. He hadn't eaten since Hardee's and even that was on the run. It would be good to eat again.

"Hi, Jonathan," said a female voice from behind him.

He whirled in his seat and saw a pretty blonde waitress standing beside him, face aglow. Her color-coordinated blouse and jumper matched the decor of the bar but couldn't hide her attractive figure. "I am really glad you decided to come back, Jonathan," she said, opening her order pad. "What can I get for you?" When she looked up from her pad, their eyes met.

Ahmay scrunched up his eyebrows and stared hard at the waitress. "Jonathan is in transition shock," he said gently, "and needs a little food to get his bearings."

Jonathan sat temporarily inert, transfixed by the woman.

"He will have turkey, mashed potatoes, and honey biscuits," said Ahmay, a slight irritation creeping into his voice. "Also, bring us a couple of moon teas."

The waitress nodded and walked away.

Jonathan stared after her. Something about her haunted him, but he couldn't focus. Too much was happening at once.

A few feet away, the waitress turned around and met Jonathan's stare. The two looked into each other's souls for a brief second. He wasn't positive, but he was almost sure he knew her from some other time and place.

Ahmay grunted. "Once you have had some nourishment," he said, "you will understand this place better." He pointed at his head. "When you live in here, it is hard to always know. When you live in here," he said, patting his chest, "it is always easier."

Jonathan shook his head from side to side. "There's nothing easy about this place," he said, taking a deep breath. "I'd just like to know where I am, for Pete's sake. And how come everyone knows my name, but I don't know theirs? Who was that woman?"

Ahmay spread his big hands and fingers, palms down. "I know you are upset, Jonathan. Everything will become clear after you have eaten. Why not just relax for a few minutes until your food gets here? I am sorry we got off on the wrong foot."

"Me, too," said Jonathan, looking around the room for a second time. "This certainly is one of the most unusual bars I've been to."

His eyes were drawn back to the shields on the walls. Each had a different insignia: some looked like Egyptian hieroglyphics, others like Chinese or Japanese writings. He spotted one that looked as if it were drawn by Native Americans. On his far left, he noticed one shield with green and deep-violet light behind it. On the front of the shield were triangles with lines running through them. It reminded him of smoothed–out lightning bolts. To the left and the right of this shield were two identical and unusual shapes; Jonathan imagined them to be bookends. In the upper right-hand corner, was a small emblem composed of several loops, side–by–side and inter–looped.

He studied the shield, trying to decide if he dare ask Ahmay another question and risk another answer he didn't understand. He still wasn't sure if he should stay in this place; it felt good to be here, but he was still worried about that guy who'd been chasing him and his feeling of impending doom. It hadn't left completely, although it seemed to have dissipated slightly.

While he pondered, his eyes drifted across the room to the far end of the bar. Several doors lined the wall. He turned to face Ahmay; a faint grin played at the corners of the tall man's mouth.

"Do those doors lead to banquet rooms?"

Ahmay cleared his throat. "In a manner of speaking."

"Could you be more specific?"

"I could," he said, nodding, "but it would not be fair to you because you would not understand my words. When the time is right, we will visit the rooms behind those doors, and then you will understand and maybe even know."

"Know what? Why are you always so vague?"

The waitress walked up, carrying Jonathan's food. "Here is your order," she said, spreading it out on the table. Her hand gently brushed against his.

His heart almost jumped out of his chest.

"You know, Jonathan," she continued, a big smile on her face, "we have a lot of catching up to do. Let us get together for a chat at the end of my shift?"

Jonathan looked up at the beautiful woman. A sudden rush of memories and emotions filled his senses: he knew her. Very well.

Ahmay grunted and glared at the woman. "You know better, young lady. I told you we were not to be in your station."

As the tall man and the waitress talked, Jonathan's mind raced elsewhere. He was seeing or experiencing a new phenomenon: it was as if several videos about him and this woman were fast–forwarding simultaneously through his consciousness. He saw the two of them together. Some of the scenes had a strange familiarity, and then thoughts and emotions long-forgotten flooded in, only to be erased as new scenes flashed by. Occasionally, bits of conversations between them played dimly in the background, only to be drowned by the new feelings in his heart.

"I am sorry, Ahmay," she continued, momentarily ignoring Jonathan, "I just could not help myself. When I saw him ... "

"I understand," Ahmay interrupted, "but he needs to focus on other things right now. Give us a little time together ... "

"Ashle," said a powerful voice, sounding as if it came through a PA. "Please report immediately to conference room number four with Diane."

The woman's cheery expression changed and she sighed. "Excuse me, Jonathan," she said. "I have to go." She started to leave, then turned back toward him. "Remember what I said."

He was still focused on the images in his mind. Realizing that she was leaving, "I will," was all he could think to blurt out.

As she moved away, he noticed the grace with which she walked—like no woman he had ever known. Yet he did know her; he was sure of that. He studied her and tried to remember. He guessed that she was in her late twenties and stood about five-eight—taller than either Ruth or Judy. The woman's natural blonde hair was tied up in a bun, fully exposing her milky–white, flawless complexion. He noticed again that her uniform, although designed to de–emphasize her figure, couldn't hide all her curves.

Stop it, Taylor, he told himself. You're being watched. Okay—you've seen that you made love with her and it was wonderful, but that's no reason to leer. Now if you could only remember her name, the one you knew her by. It wasn't Ashle or Diane. It's ... a P word, something from the Bible, like Peter or Paul. That's it: Paula. I knew her as Paula.

The images began to come back.

"Jonathan," ordered Ahmay, jolting him back to the booth in the bar, "do you not want to try some of the moon tea? It will help."

"I know her," he blurted. "I know her; her name's Paula. I really know that woman."

"You are right," Ahmay said, laughing at him again. "There is a lot more that you know but have forgotten. Your knowing will increase exponentially as soon as you eat some food."

"There you go again with the vague answers. If I eat this food, will you stop that, too?"

"My answers are not meant to be vague. I am trying to give you answers equal to your knowing at the moment. The more you eat and the more we talk, the more will be your knowing. Your focus has been on other perspectives and realities, but soon you will know the many things of which I speak."

"How about something simple," Jonathan asked, "like, where the heck am I?" He realized this was not like him— to be so confrontational with a stranger. What's come over me? "Is this place real or am I dreaming?" he continued. "And what about that guy who chased me in here—what happened to him? He should have come in the door by now; he was right behind me."

Ahmay smiled knowingly. "You are a seeker and a traveler, Jonathan," he said. "That is why you came in here. A big part of you enjoys the unknown journey, the excitement. Most times, the destination is of no importance to you. Only Bears who have spent many journeys outside the cave can see that. You are like the Bear who has been wandering Mother Earth and has grown weary. Now you need to hibernate. That is why you have chosen to return to the cave."

"What are you talking about? Bears and Mother Earth? You sound like an ad for a PBS special or something." He paused. "I've got to eat this food; the suspense is making me nuts." He reached for his fork and knife. "By the way, Ahmay, do you know that I've got an audition in an hour or so?"

The Indian nodded and lightly touched Jonathan's arm. "Try and focus on this moment, as it has much to teach you. Do not worry, we will be done in plenty of time for your audition," he said. "Before you eat, though, you need to remember to give thanks—something you have forgotten how to do."

"Give thanks? What for? Is this some kind of religious dream brought on by a need for acceptance by my mother?"

"This is no dream, Jonathan," Ahmay said quietly. "This is much more than a dream. This is Reality, a Reality well beyond your realities, but nevertheless, Reality. Now, please, give thanks and eat. Your knowing is about to exceed your dreams."

Chapter 6

"An aching or painful void sits at your core, seeking relief."

Jonathan wanted to scream. Give thanks? he thought. Every time I hear those words, all I can think of is my mother and those nuns of South Chicago—tough, mean, and controlling. I wonder if that's what Ahmay is all about: controlling. He certainly acts that way sometimes.

It is true, though, Taylor, that you've forgotten how to give thanks. But then, it's also true that the concepts of religion and personal philosophy and spirituality have all become one confused muddle for you. One of the things you have become aware of lately is that you can have spirituality without religious affiliation; the two are not interdependent. That was a major breakthrough. After all those years of Catholic education, not once can you remember making or feeling a spiritual connection with God. Pretty sad, Taylor. Time to start.

Jonathan made the sign of the cross. "Thanks God," he said and began to eat.

Ahmay smiled. "Good job, young Bear," he said, "I know that was hard for you, but it was an important first step." He watched his guest eat for a few moments. "It was also a sign of a small level of trust. That was very nice. Thank you."

"You're welcome," Jonathan said with his mouth full.

"I am your companion here. The more you trust me, the more answers I can share and help you understand. If you want to hasten the process, then there is a way we can do that, too."

"How?" asked Jonathan, sipping tea.

"Complete trust."

"What do you mean?"

Ahmay pointed at Jonathan's hands. "Put them on the table."

He did.

"I am going to touch your hands. If you do not like what happens, pull your hands away. Understand?"

Jonathan nodded.

Ahmay placed his huge, weathered hands over Jonathan's. The visitor from San Diego began to feel dizzy. He closed his eyes. It was as if he were standing on the top of a very tall mountain; there was a strong wind blowing around him. He felt like he was going to fall, and then it was like he was having a dream about flying. He was gliding on the wind—he was a bird. He looked over at his wings. He was an eagle and there was another eagle with him—bigger and stronger and wiser, but he felt like he was going to fall.

"You are safe," came the words into his mind.

The landscape below seemed lush and beautiful; the sky was clear and warm. It was so peaceful and silent, he felt like he wanted to fly by himself. He flapped his wings, and then the other eagle was gone. He felt so free, something he'd always dreamed of—actually flying. Flying? How could he be flying? He wasn't a bird. He's a person. Now the landscape rose up; he was falling.

On the ground, two dark craters appeared. They were getting bigger and bigger, closer and closer; he couldn't stop. He began to quiver with fear; he was going to die. Suddenly, the other eagle appeared at his side, and his plummet stopped. He flapped his wings. Once again, it was peaceful and silent in the sky.

Ahmay took his hands away.

Jonathan saw darkness and then heard the sounds of the bar. He opened his eyes. He wasn't dizzy any more, but his adrenaline was pumping hard. Ahmay's deep brown eyes stared at him. "What was that?" asked Jonathan, hands shaking.

Ahmay shrugged. "Drink your tea; you will feel better."

The younger man shook his head. "I feel great. I've just never had anything like that happen to me before. It was exciting and scary all at the same time. Who are you?"

The older man laughed. "I told you."

Jonathan sipped some tea. "I know what you said, but I'm not sure I understand. Companion for what? This is no ordinary bar and you're no ordinary Shoshone."

"You are right," said Ahmay, still smiling, "but you are changing the subject. Before I gave you that little demonstration, we were talking about trust. How do you feel about that? Do you feel as though you can trust me enough so we can take some shortcuts? Are you willing to suspend your natural disbelief and take what I say on face value?"

Jonathan rocked his head back and forth, then began nodding. "Yes, I think I can, but I'm still going to ask questions."

"That is appropriate and as it should be," said Ahmay, his face turning serious. "What questions do you have in mind?"

"Let's go back to the bear and the cave you mentioned before," said Jonathan. "Why does the bear return?"

"Because it is home. It is a place where questions are answered, the void filled, the path of life made brighter. It is where the body, mind, and heart can become more intimately connected to the spirit."

"Is that what this place is, my cave?"

Ahmay chuckled. "You might say that; it is also much more."

Jonathan took a deep breath. "That food really hit the spot." He sipped more tea. "So, how did I find this place?"

"As with so many questions," said Ahmay, pushing his hair back out of his eyes, "the answer is within. What have you been working on lately in your life? "

"My music, mostly, and I've been trying to relax my body by doing breathing and stretching exercises. I even tried yoga. And ever since I've been in San Diego, I've been working hard on trying to say what I think and express what I feel, especially when it comes to anger ... " He paused, searching his memory. "Lately, I've been meditating whenever I can."

Ahmay nodded and smiled. "You see, without knowing it you have answered your own question. You told me you are working on your body, mind, heart, and soul. I have been watching you slowly drift to the place of Silence. When you moved west to San Diego, you allowed the Four Winds to blow freely, without interference; the Silence and the Winds have enabled you to find this place."

"Is this place real?" Jonathan asked, pushing his empty plates to one side.

"Your focus is your reality!" Ahmay exclaimed, almost yelling. "Where are you focused at this very moment?"

Jonathan frowned. "Here in the Celestial Bar, in this booth, with you yelling at me."

"And before that?"

"In the park with some crazy guy chasing me?"

"And before that?"

Jonathan paused. "Ah–h–h," he said, trying to remember; he'd almost forgotten. "In Los Angeles ... napping before my audition at Warner Studios. Actually, when I fell asleep, I was trying to focus on my breathing—meditating."

"Is being in L.A. real?"

Jonathan nodded.

"Is this place real? Was it real when you became an eagle?"

He squirmed in his seat and scratched his head. "I don't know. My flying seemed real at the time. This place seems real because you say it's real and I believe you. So, yes, I guess it's real."

"Ah–hah," Ahmay smiled. "Now you are beginning to explore the different levels of realities, or should I say, consciousness. Remember, there is a big difference between your consciousness—or reality—and Divine Reality."

"Divine Reality—what's that?"

"Divine Reality just is, no more, no less. It has been and is and will be occurring every moment of all eternity. The Divine Reality is manifested in a multitude of ways throughout the universe. One way is through the physical universe, but such manifestations are merely reflections of the Divine Reality."

Jonathan stared at his companion. "So what does Divine Reality have to do with my reality?"

Ahmay grinned. "Imagine an all–encompassing Divine Reality as would be represented by a huge, blazing star. From that star shoot innumerable rays of light out into limitless space. Each ray of light is comprised by more innumerable particles of light. Each particle of light represents one soul. The further these particles move away from the star, the more they forget their connection to the Source. Because of this disorientation, they begin to move off in search of the Source. That is the driving force behind all life, what I call the Movement."

"And that includes me?" asked Jonathan.

"Not exactly. There is much more. Picture yourself as one of these particles of light. You enter a room called Earth; on the walls are three different mirrors called Physical, Emotional, and Intellectual. As you look into these mirrors, you see a short you, a handsome you, a disfigured you; an angry you, a loving you, a frightened you; a smart you, a curious you, or an ignorant you."

"Okay," Jonathan said, "so if I'm this soul and I see the essence of me viewed through all this disorientation, what's that have to do with Jonathan Taylor?"

Ahmay slowly rubbed his big hands together. "The longer and more intensely a soul focuses on its own physical, emotional, and intellectual reflections, the more those reflections will appear real. That is just as much a challenge for you as anyone else. The difficulty for Jonathan Taylor is that what you see of reality is no more real than a good movie on Earth is an accurate representation of life on Earth. The missing component is Spirituality. Spirituality is the essence of who you are in spirit and soul—your connection to the Source or Divine Reality."

Ahmay took a deep breath. "And now, back to your original question. What you call your reality is in actuality your focus—or your awareness or your consciousness—of the reflections of the Divine Reality. And those reflections are only real in that they are an integral part of the Divine Reality. But, without Divine Reality, your reality could not exist."

"So is there any hope for me," asked Jonathan, "or am I just another lost soul?"

"There is much hope, but first you have to see how you have been working against yourself."

"How's that?"

"For most of your life, you have seen yourself as a mirrored reflection known as Jonathan Taylor, only son of Mr. and Mrs. Taylor, therapist, husband, restaurant owner, Catholic, jock, musician and composer, and depending upon your experience here, possible movie-score writer. Because your focus has been primarily within just those reflections, your life on Earth has been lacking in fulfillment. An aching or painful void sits at your core, seeking relief."

Jonathan was silent. He was feeling vulnerable and anxious. Something was happening to him here in the Celestial Bar, and he wasn't sure if it was in his mind or if it was real. He was having a hard time concentrating on everything Ahmay said because every few minutes he thought he felt that same feeling of foreboding that chased him in the bar in the first place.

"You all right?" asked Ahmay.

Jonathan nodded. "I'm listening."

"Many people who feel that painful void tend to think and act in reaction to their mirrored focus. To fill that void, these people seek relief in other forms of the same painful void, such as new relationships, more money, a new city, or the acquisition of more things. But that never brings the fulfillment they seek; they end up feeling even more disconnected. That is what happened to you, right?"

Jonathan shrugged. "I guess so. I'm not really sure. I'm trying to digest this stuff and there's a lot to think about. You're right about my feelings of disconnectedness. I just never knew what to call them, but I knew something was missing."

"I understand," said Ahmay. "The trick to grasping the concept of replacing the painful void with spirituality is to remember that Divine Reality is multi–dimensional, with spirituality at its very core. The first step toward understanding is to see beyond the reflected images in the mirrors. You have to see yourself and the universe as bigger than those limiting reflections. The universe and you are much more—more expansive, or what I would call multi–dimensional."

"All this thinking," interrupted Jonathan, "has got me really thirsty. Can we order something cold to drink?"

"In a minute," Ahmay said. "We are going to take a walk to the workout rooms. On the way, we can get something at the bar." He looked Jonathan in the eye, studying him like an eagle watching its offspring eat. "Remember, I realize how hard it is for you to do these things. Your life on Earth is basically a school where, like so many other schools, the courses are extremely difficult because there are so many reflected images to understand and see beyond. You, and the rest of your classmates, did not choose an easy school."

Jonathan felt like he'd heard Ahmay's words before. It was as if another set of videos were about to start playing in his head, similar to when Paula touched his hand. Wonder what happened to her? he thought. She wanted to see me at the end of her shift, whenever that is. Maybe she'll be able to help me remember. Somehow these memories seem to be locked in my heart, not my head. Maybe deeper than that; maybe even in my soul.

"Can we get that drink now?" he asked. "My throat's so dry, I swear we're in the middle of Death Valley."

"Good idea," Ahmay said, sliding from the booth and leading the way. "There is someone I want you to meet. You will like him."

Jonathan felt his anxiety rising. As they approached the long bar, his eyes were drawn to a tall, well–built man working behind it. Despite having the muscle tone of someone in his twenties, crow's feet beside each eye and streaks of gray in his otherwise brown hair told Jonathan that this man was probably fortyish. He guessed the man stood at least six-three and weighed in at about 225; might even be ex–linebacker material.

"Mr. Taylor," the tall, slender Native American said, "I would like to introduce you to a friend of mine."

Jonathan smiled and extended his hand toward the man behind the bar. "Nice to meet you, Zorinthalian."

Wait a minute, Taylor. Where did that come from? You know his name and you've never met this man before in your life.

"Same here, Jonathan," Zorinthalian said in a deep voice, shaking hands. He served Jonathan a cold glass of water and Ahmay an envelope.

How'd he know my name and that I was thirsty? Jonathan wondered as he disengaged from the man's powerful grip. Conflicting energies coursed through his mind and body. When he shook hands with Zorinthalian, he felt a great loving presence, almost as if they were brothers or related somehow. His consciousness was immediately overrun with scenes from other times and places when the two of them had laughed, fought, cried, and shared experiences. The colors and smells of an ancient place swept across his mind.

Simultaneously, Jonathan felt a great negative force; it was very close and seemed to be gaining strength. If he didn't know better, he would have sworn this negative energy was coming from Zorinthalian. But that couldn't be possible: he felt an unexplainable friendship for this man. Jonathan looked at the other people in the bar. There was nothing distinctive about any of them. They all seemed harmless enough. The only people nearby were Ahmay and some grubby–looking barback. Jonathan decided to speak about all this with Ahmay when there weren't so many other people around.

"The food must be working," Ahmay said to Zorinthalian, gesturing at Jonathan with the envelope. He turned and walked down the hallway toward the row of doors. "Come on, little Bear, you do not have much time, and you definitely need a workout."

"Thanks for the water," Jonathan said to Zorinthalian.

"Any time," said the gentle hulk of a man.

Jonathan followed Ahmay as they walked past doors marked Conference Rooms 1, 2, 3, and 4. Wasn't Paula in Conference Room 4 with Diane? Maybe he could get a minute or so alone with her at some point. He'd have to figure a way to get away from Ahmay.

The two men came to another hallway and turned right. Now the doors were marked "Transition Room" with ascending numbers. They stopped outside Transition Room 6. "See this envelope?" asked Ahmay.

Jonathan nodded yes.

The Native American knocked on the door. "This envelope contains disks I got from the library. I think you will find them very interesting."

There was no answer to Ahmay's knock. He opened the door and went in.

Jonathan followed. To him the room had a homey, welcoming feel, with more unusual, soft lighting like in the bar. The carpeted room looked to be about thirty-by-thirty feet, with several chairs, a couch, and a recliner for furniture. He sat down in the recliner. "I thought we were going to a workout room," he said, removing his running shoes. There were pebbles in them that had bothered him ever since he ran into the park.

"This *is* a workout room," said Ahmay. "In here, you can stretch and become more flexible; you can also become stronger. When you are in transition, that is when you truly work out."

Jonathan thought about pointing out to Ahmay that the word "workout" had a different meaning for him than it did for Jonathan, but he decided to save his breath. He looked around the room. On one wall, an equipment center appeared to contain a VCR, radio, CD player, video disc player, computer keyboard and screen, control panel, plus other electronic gadgets he had never seen before.

Ahmay opened the envelope, pulled out what looked like an under–sized CD, and placed it in the CD player.

Piano music began to play, a concerto Jonathan had never heard before. It sounded like Mozart, but he knew it wasn't. The sound system was the best he had ever heard, too. It was so good, it felt as if he were playing the piano. The resonance tingled in his fingers, hands, and arms. He felt soothed—almost as if he had been drugged but still fully aware of events in the room.

Relax, Taylor. Quit fighting it. Roll with the flow. Who knows where all this is leading; you have to let go. You're not in L.A. and you're not playing the piano, even though it may feel that way. It doesn't matter. What matters is that this Ahmay guy likes you for some reason and he's trying to help you. So listen to what he has to say. It can't hurt and it might help. Don't forget you've got an audition in an hour or so. Maybe what's happening here will produce a way to fix the problem with your music and your finger. Nah, that's just wishful thinking. You can't fix real problems in a dream. What a dream, though!

Ahmay's a piece of work. Never met a Native American so friendly and wise and good–humored. 'Course, truth is you haven't known that many Native Americans, period. The few you've known were in Chicago and Florida, and they were just passing shadows in your life. You've never really had one as a friend. And then there's that Zorinthalian guy. My God, what a horse! I wouldn't want to meet him in a dark alley, but he doesn't seem like the threatening type. I know him from somewhere, but I'll be darned if I can remember. This is so bizarre. I feel as though we're like brothers: I know his name—and I don't know why—from some unknown portion of my past. But, when? I can account for all the years of my life and there was no Zorinthalian. Not by that name or any other. I would have remembered. And then there was that unbelievable feeling I got when he shook my hand. I've never felt so calm and peaceful and loved as a friend as I did at that instant. That's crazy.

And what about that Paula? My God, is she ever beautiful! I know her. We've made love and we've been best friends. That blows my mind. How can I feel as though I know her so well and yet I barely remember her name? When could I have known her? Not in Chicago and not in Florida and certainly not in California. That feeling of imminent danger seems to have subsided for the moment. I wish I knew how to fix that problem. Since Ahmay can read my mind, I wonder if he knows what I'm thinking this very moment?

Ahmay was still adjusting the equipment on the wall. He twisted a few knobs, then punched two buttons in rapid succession. A tiny light appeared in the wall to Jonathan's left. It was a pinhole of light coming out of the wall about three feet off the ground and shooting, uninterrupted, to the opposite wall, where it became a large circle, almost reaching floor–to–ceiling.

"What's that?" Jonathan asked, still feeling woozy.

"It is a VF light," Ahmay answered matter–of–factly.

Jonathan tried to focus and formulate another question. His mind felt lazy and relaxed. It was easier to study the light beam; it reminded him of his childhood days in Chicago. He used to love to sit in the family living room and watch the dust particles floating in a beam of sunlight streaming in from the outside. These dust particles swirling around always surprised him; they were always there, but he only remembered them when he saw them in a beam of sunlight.

The VF light Ahmay had just actuated was a bright white beam of light with tiny particles rushing around in a counterclockwise fashion.

"What's VF mean?" Jonathan asked, scratching his head.

"'Vibrational frequency,'" Ahmay replied, pushing more buttons. "One of the Universal Principles is that 'Everything Is Energy', and one of its Laws is that 'All Energy Has Its Own Unique Vibrational Frequency.' You are energy and you have your own VF."

"So what?"

"So here is a chance for you to take one of those informational shortcuts we talked about earlier," said Ahmay, turning to face Jonathan.

"What?" Jonathan tried to clear his head. The piano concerto was still playing but seemed to have gotten quieter. "I don't understand what you're talking about."

"It is simple," Ahmay said. "All you have to do is step into the light. The light will measure your VF and instantly know who you are. It is similar to fingerprinting."

"And then what?"

"And then you will be able to access the Celestial Library. Among other things, it contains the history of all journeys, including yours. Actually, it has the records of all that has ever happened in this universe. It will also know—through your VF—your present level of consciousness. Each level brings a different degree of awareness."

Jonathan shook his head, still trying to focus. "Ahmay, I just don't get it. After the light knows who I am, then what? What's going to happen that'll help me?"

Ahmay laughed good–naturedly. "The light will then be able to answer more of your questions about spirituality or reflected reality in language and logic that is understandable to you. After all, what good are answers if you cannot understand them?"

Now it was beginning to make a little sense, Jonathan thought. "So how does the light know my questions? Does it read my mind or do I just say them out loud or what?"

Ahmay was still grinning. "Here is what happens: You step into the light with your whole body. Then you ask whatever questions you want, out loud. Some of your answers will be spoken, some will be in musical form, some in three-dimensional video, some virtual reality, and sometimes they will be all four simultaneously. It can get pretty intense. If you feel like it is too much, you can step out of the light and sit down and still be able to hear or see the answer. But if you want a full 'knowing,' then you should stay in the light during the whole answer."

"And where are you going to be all this time?"

"I will be right here," said Ahmay. "I am not going to leave you. Any questions you have or anything that does not make sense, you let me know. Remember, I am your companion."

Jonathan nodded. He was reassured. He studied the light for a few more minutes, then moved over beside it. Slowly, he placed his fingers in the light, then his whole hand, and finally his whole arm. Light, pastel colors appeared to come rippling out of the portion of him that was in the light. Startled, he jerked his arm and hand from the light.

Ahmay burst out in loud, raucous laughter.

"What's so funny?" barked Jonathan. "You act like I'm stupid or something for being startled. You didn't tell me about those colors."

Ahmay's laughter stopped and he frowned. "First of all," he said gently, "you are not stupid. Secondly, you already know about the colors you saw in the VF light, you just seem to have forgotten. I did not know you had forgotten so much, and that surprised me. I am sorry it appeared that I was laughing at you."

"What do you mean, I've forgotten?"

"You know much more than you realize," Ahmay said, sitting down on one of the chairs. He crossed his long legs and well–worn leather cowboy boots, pushing hair from his eyes with his callused hands. "Let me give you an example. Whenever you move, you pack things into boxes. Let us suppose for this example that one of those boxes accidentally got left in your garage under some books or furniture. Years later, you discover the box. You open it, totally surprised, forgetting where it came from and what was inside. You actually know about its contents; it just takes a few minutes for your memory to kick in."

Jonathan ran his hands through own his blond hair and down the back of his muscular neck. "How will I ever remember how much I already know?"

"That is why we came to this room. I am trying to speed up the process. That is what this VF light beam is all about: to help you remember. Before you go to Earth School, you empty your pockets of soul memory. I did not realize how much you had forgotten. For such an old soul like you to have forgotten about the colors in the VF beam struck me as just plain funny. To me, it was as if you forgot your name or your parents' nationality. I have to admit that being here at the Celestial Bar makes me forget how intense Earth focus can be. I apologize if I have offended you."

"I understand," said Jonathan. "Sorry I barked at you."

Ahmay chuckled. "Thank you, young Bear."

Jonathan scowled. "Are there any more surprises in there?" he asked, jerking his head toward the light beam.

Ahmay roared. "Of course, there are more surprises in there. The secret is to not mind the surprises, and to expect the unexpected. If you knew what to expect, then why bother with this whole exercise? Part of growth is surprise at new 'knowings.' That is half the fun." He paused, his face getting serious again. "Come on, Jonathan. Relax. This is not death or torture. This is an adventure. Just let it happen."

Chapter 7

"Balance is the natural state of the universe.... "

Jonathan took a deep breath and turned to face the beam of light coming from the wall. Carefully, he placed his hand back into it and again he saw the many colors streaming from him. "Man, this is so weird," he said to Ahmay, "I don't know if I'll ever get used to it."

"You will be just fine," said Ahmay. "I will stick around for a little while before I go and chat with Zorinthalian. If you need me, just call and I will be here."

Jonathan nodded his understanding, then eased his whole body into the light. Immediately, he felt as if he were in a different world; his only consciousness was of the light. The fact that he was in the Celestial Bar in a special Transition Room with Ahmay shifted to the recesses of his thoughts; his concentration was on the light. It became his only focus.

A faint but pleasant tingling sensation raced through his body, and he looked down at his midsection to see what was happening. It was as if he could see through himself to his backbone. There was a reddish hue coming from the base of his spine, and then he noticed an orange glow coming from just below his bellybutton and a yellow light from his solar plexus.

"What's going on?" he asked.

"Please be more specific," said a precise male voice in a low register.

Jonathan frowned and worked hard to bring Ahmay back to the forefront of his thoughts. He looked over at him sitting on the couch, legs crossed. That was not Ahmay's voice, he told himself; his voice is lighter and more poetic. Besides sounding officious, this new voice resonated throughout Jonathan's body like certain special low notes on the stereo or at the symphony. This unfamiliar voice had to be someone new. "Who are you?" Jonathan asked, turning his attention back to the many colors streaming from his body.

"I am Ramda."

"Where are you?"

"Here in the light with you."

"But I can't see you."

"True, but I am here nonetheless. The Divine Reality does not depend upon sight for confirmation of a truth."

Jonathan was puzzled. "Why are you here with me?"

"I am your interface with the Celestial Library," Ramda said. "My purpose is to access information you request, then present the answer in a way that will enable your knowing."

"Okay," said Jonathan, looking around at the light beam and the rainbow of colors flowing from his body, "what's happening to me at this very moment?"

"Nothing."

"What do you mean?"

"Nothing is happening *to* you."

"Then what are all these colors about?"

"They are not happening *to* you; they *are* you," Ramda said. "What you are seeing—in a hazy sort of way—is your ethereal body. You might call it a particle of light, your soul."

"So what's the light doing?"

"Reflecting what is already there." Ramda paused. "Let me place before you a reflection device, much like what you would call a mirror. This device will reflect back to you what you are currently allowing yourself to see."

Instantly, a full–length shiny apparatus appeared inside the light beam right in front of Jonathan. In it, he saw the same red, orange, and yellow hues flowing from his fully–clothed body. However, this time he could see more colors than before: green light was coming from his chest area, sky–blue encircled his throat, indigo hovered at the back of his head, violet floated over the crown of his skull. The trouble was that the colors all seemed to be lacking definition or clarity.

Jonathan remembered a trick that he'd seen people use to view camouflaged three-dimensional pictures. They call it "looking beyond" or "through" to pull the 3-D image into focus. They focus their gaze on the outside perimeter of the page and if they do it correctly, the "hidden" image magically "appears" in several dimensions. He decided to try this technique with Ramda's reflecting device.

At first, everything appeared a blur, nondescript and interwoven, but after a few minutes, the colors began to localize. The new way of focusing worked. He looked directly at his own reflection: a faint, blue light surrounded his whole body.

"What do you mean when you say soul?" Jonathan asked.

"It is your spirit body," answered Ramda.

"What about it?"

"It is always with you. In fact," said Ramda, "your soul is much more of you than you may have realized. The physical part of you is but a mere reflection of your soul. So to answer your question, your soul is you. However, at this moment, you are only able to see portions of your spirit body."

Jonathan frowned, trying to think. "What is the significance of the colors I do see in your reflecting device?"

"They are energy conduit centers. For you the easiest explanation I can think of is to tell you that they—the colors you see as you stand in this beam of light—are the glue between your body and spirit. They are what enable you to move in this physical world and still be in contact with your spirit."

"But why are there so many different colors? Why aren't they all the same?"

"The red light at the base of your spine resonates with your physicalness and your survival aspects, the orange with your creativity and sexuality, and the yellow from your solar plexus with your intellect and power. The green is for your heart."

"Then why do I see some pink around my heart area; what does that mean?"

"Hmmm," said Ramda. "You are very observant, Jonathan. Good question. There are many colors associated with each of the centers. At this point, I am only telling you the basic light energies. Because each person is different, each would require different VF's to effect an adjustment. Pink happens to be more of a feminine energy but excellent for you: it helps you with balance—something we will talk more about later. Specifically, pink means that there are openings in the walls around your heart, the walls you use to protect yourself from emotional hurt. This pink that you are seeing is your color for sharing love in an intimate relationship."

Jonathan sighed. So much was happening, it was hard for him to think about everything at once. Intimate relationship? Who could that be? Paula. He felt his heart skip a beat: he remembered that he was going to try and see her when he and Ahmay walked down the corridor past Conference Room 4. He wanted to reconnect with her, especially about all the things they had been to each other on another day in another place. He missed her.

He looked down at his heart area. Already, the color pink was getting darker.

"You all right?" asked Ramda.

Jonathan nodded.

"Let us continue. The sky–blue color around your throat resonates your expression of self. If ever your throat feels tight, ask yourself what in your heart or mind is not being expressed. There is an Energy Law that states 'All Energy Must Flow.' This principle must be at work in order for this particular conduit center to function in balance.

"The third eye center is indicated by the color indigo; it stimulates your intuition and connection with your multi–dimensional aspects.

"The color violet above the crown of your head indicates your connection point with your spirituality and God."

To Jonathan, all these colors seemed like a lot to think about, but now, thanks to Ramda, they were becoming more manageable. At the mention of the top of his head, he glanced into the reflection device and saw new things above his head, more conduit centers. They were very small and faint and colorless. A ray of light was emanating from the top of his head. It began with a narrow beam and broadened as it moved upward.

"What's going on there just above my head?" he asked.

"More conduit centers," Ramda replied. "They connect you with different aspects of yourself and the universe. You will work with those energies, but not right now; you need to be more in balance. First, you need to work on your day–to–day connections. There is much to do."

Jonathan nodded and kept looking into the reflection device. "Sure would be nice if my mirror at home worked this way."

"It could," said Ramda.

"I've never seen anything like this in my mirror."

"What were you looking for?"

"My body."

"And that is what you saw," Ramda said. "Your focus was there. You limited your vision and therefore could not see your spiritual self. It is just a habit, one you can change."

Jonathan stood there, watching the reflections. The more he "looked beyond" the device, the greater the clarity and intensity of the colors. The moment he began to think about what was happening, the colors seemed to diminish and disappear.

"When that happens," he asked, assuming that Ramda knew what he had been thinking, "is that part of the Universal Principles?"

Ramda chuckled. "That is excellent, Jonathan," he said. "Acting on your new–found awareness is encouraging. Most of the time I do know what you are thinking; emotions are where I have problems—they do not lend themselves to quantification. In any event, congratulations on being willing to try out a new consciousness."

"Thank you," said Jonathan, pleased with himself.

"To answer your question," Ramda continued, "yes. The colors you saw, which are a reflection of your soul, are governed by the Universal Principles."

"Would you explain to me about Universal Principles?"

Without warning, the reflection device disappeared and was immediately replaced by another piece of equipment. This one was much bigger, and its clear plastic screen sparkled in the beam of light coming from the wall. The device stood a little higher than Jonathan and was about six feet wide; it reminded him of a huge interactive computer screen. The screen's background was a vibrant purple and printed across the top in gold letters were the words: "Explain to me about Universal Principles." Centered underneath were the words, "Universal Principles," with four separate dialogue boxes. Each one was headed by a different statement. They read: "Everything Is Energy"; "All Energy Is Interconnected"; "Energy Just Is"; "Energy Always Moves Toward Balance."

Jonathan didn't say a word, but decided to touch the dialogue box marked "Everything Is Energy." The screen changed to indicate more choices. He soon realized the computer was capable of providing endless, in–depth historical, cultural, and scientific information about energy.

For instance, one subcategory under "Western Scientific" ended with the statement: "With the advent of the electron microscope, man could finally see that the basic building blocks of the universe are actually in constant motion. The universe, when broken down to its simplest form, is truly nothing more than pure energy."

"I do not expect you to memorize all the information on the screen, Jonathan," said Ramda. "It is just there in case you decide you need it to help you understand Universal Principles."

Jonathan nodded and pushed "Return." The screen returned to its original state. He then touched the dialogue box marked, "All Energy is Interconnected." What followed was another comprehensive discussion of the subject, including the Unified Field Theory, Einstein's Theory of Relativity, the Chaos Theory, the Hologram Theory, Quantum Mechanics, and even the Hundredth Monkey Principle, where information or energy is exchanged between species regardless of distance, resulting in a critical mass expansion of consciousness.

One paragraph in this subsection stuck in Jonathan's mind: "In the late 20th century, with the advent of quantum physics, the scientific community moved from describing the universe and humans as simply composites of atoms to 'ever–changing energy fields.' The perspective of humankind's existence changed from a universe of parts, things, or objects to an ever–changing 'Whole of Interconnected Energies.' Thus, each person is connected to every other person, to nature, to the planet, and to the universe. The universe is a Whole, comprised of energies that interact, share, and create."

He pressed "Return," ready to continue his next intellectual exploration on this special piece of hardware. He felt invigorated and curiosity had taken over his every thought and deed. If everything is energy, he wondered to himself, how is one supposed to tell one energy form from another?

"The same way I can identify you," Ramda interrupted, "by VF—vibrational frequency."

The screen in front of Jonathan flashed a new image which read: "All energies have their own unique vibrational frequency." There was another dialogue box with the following menu: "Physical," "Emotional," "Intellectual," "Spiritual," and "Personal Examples." He pointed at the last one.

Immediately, amorphous images appeared on the screen, quickly replaced by colors of the rainbow. Along the right edge, centered in the middle from bottom to top, were the colors red, orange, yellow, green, blue, indigo, and violet. Along the left edge of the screen were numbers.

"What do those numbers mean?" asked Jonathan.

"They represent vibrational frequencies. Notice how the numbers increase, bottom to top, as the colors change, bottom to top, from red to violet."

"Some numbers on the top left edge of the screen don't have any corresponding colors on the right edge of the screen. Why is that?" asked Jonathan.

"What you are seeing on the right of the screen is a spectrum of light. Where you do not see any colors corresponding to the vibrational frequencies on the left, there actually exist energies that are outside the perceptions of the human eye, such as X–rays and gamma rays. This is a visual manifestation of the fact that there are realities outside the five human senses."

Jonathan widened his eyes. "Oh, I see. Kind of like dogs' ability to hear compared to that of humans. The sounds are there, it's just that humans can't hear them."

"Exactly," said Ramda.

The rainbow colors disappeared and a kettledrum came into view. Jonathan touched it with his middle finger. A low, hollow "waaahmp" sound filled the air, and then the drum began to play itself in a soft rhythmic beat. Next came a violin that played the dominant melody, then an oboe and a flute spinning gentle counter-harmonies. Several other musical instruments appeared before, finally, a piano appeared. He touched it and listened as it picked up the theme from the violin and improvised several new counter-melodies, all of which led back to the major theme through a series of bridges and key changes.

Jonathan realized he was hearing music as he never had before: he could focus on one instrument, several at once, or the whole ensemble. It was what he always tried to do when he was writing his own music—but here, he was actually doing it! As he focused on each instrument or group thereof, he felt a different and distinct feeling: the drums made him feel primal or physical, the piano introspective, the violin emotional, the flute ethereal or spiritual.

He noticed that along the left border of the screen, were numbers, VF's—vibrational frequencies—of the musical instruments. Without warning, the images on the screen changed, but the music continued in the background. First a boulder appeared, then a hot, macadam road, a heavenly bamboo plant, a golden retriever , and lastly, a human. Each new image showed a higher VF. After the appearance of the human figure, the screen showed the figure and its VF coming together and melding into one.

Next, Jonathan saw his own image and VF on the screen. It then became a four–dimensional view of himself, with four distinct VF groupings and colors: red, green, yellow, and violet.

"Do you understand what you see?" asked Ramda.

"I think so," Jonathan said. "When I first stepped into your light beam, I saw these colors."

"That is exactly correct," said Ramda, "as far as it goes. When you first stepped into my beam of light, we were talking about colors of the energy conduit centers; now we are talking about colors of energy systems. You are composed of four distinct energy systems which, for the purposes of this exercise, are in turn represented by different colors: physical—represented by the color red; emotional—green; intellectual—yellow; spiritual—violet. Individually, each one of these energy systems has its own

VF. Put together, these four systems create a fifth VF that forms your own individual identity, which your world calls Jonathan Taylor. You are your own unique energy, while at the same time you are connected to the whole of all energy, or Divine Reality. And that whole concept is one example of a Universal Principle."

Jonathan nodded. "I think I understand."

"Now that you think you understand," Ramda said, "here comes the most important part."

"What's that?"

"Watch the screen."

The screen went blank and the music stopped. The four colors appeared in the form of large rectangles with their appropriate VF readings superimposed over each color.

"As you can see," Ramda continued, "you are out of balance; your physical, emotional, and intellectual aspects are much more dominant than your spiritual."

Jonathan nodded and took a deep breath. It was beginning to make sense. That empty ache that he'd been carrying around all these years finally had a name. The ache of discontent that had driven him from Chicago to Key West to San Diego. The same reason he'd forgotten how to give thanks for his food: he'd abandoned his own spirituality. He saw it in other people and even Mary, the waitress at Hardee's, but for him it was nothing more than an intellectual exercise—something to be thought about and carefully considered. He hadn't wanted to jump back into another confusing and guilt-ridden hell like what he'd been through with religion. But now he could see the error of his ways. Spirituality was something he needed to work on; without it he was less than he could be and that was bad.

"Faulty logic," interrupted Ramda. "Operator error."

"What?" Jonathan said. "Who do you think you are, intruding into my personal thoughts?"

"We have more information to cover," said Ramda. "You cannot make decisions with incomplete data."

"What are you talking about?"

The screen flashed and the words "Energy Just Is." appeared.

"Why do you always talk in riddles?" Jonathan pleaded.

"Why do you stop listening? At Ahmay's request, I am here to help you understand more about the Celestial Bar and yourself. I cannot do that effectively unless you let me finish the answer to your question about Universal Principles."

"Sorry," said Jonathan, "I thought you had finished."

"Let us talk about what is on the screen: 'Energy Just Is.'"

"That's exactly what Ahmay told me about Divine Reality," said Jonathan. "Does that mean Divine Reality and Energy are the same thing?"

Ramda was silent for a moment. "Yes and no. Let me explain. All energy exists at different vibrational frequencies, but it is all interconnected by the Divine Reality. Therefore, Energy and Divine Reality are, in the final analysis, the same. That make sense?"

"I think so," Jonathan nodded.

"Now, back to 'Energy Just Is.' If there were no people on Earth, who would determine what was good and bad? For example, what if one subatomic particle smashed into another, or if one amoeba ate another organism, or if a lion killed and ate an antelope, or if a shark ate a seal, or if the ocean provided fresh fish for some and drowned others? In the heavens, stars are colliding, being born, and going nova; are those good or bad events? Each is another example of energy, and each event is a part of the Divine Reality. The question of good or bad only comes as a result of humankind. Do you agree?"

Jonathan shrugged. "I don't know. I think it's more complicated than that."

"You are right," said Ramda. "That was an insightful answer; the question I pose is more complicated than that. However, like the line from a song called 'Nights in White Satin,' will you not agree that humans do 'decide what is right and what is an illusion?'" They may be accurate and they may be inaccurate, but they do render judgments. Is that not a correct statement?"

"That is a correct statement."

"And that is precisely my point. By passing judgment, they are limiting themselves and others. More specifically, I interrupted you while you were telling yourself that without spirituality you were bad. I would like to have you consider rephrasing that statement to be 'without spirituality, Jonathan Taylor is out of balance.'"

Jonathan's eyes widened. "Balance? What does that mean?"

"The final Universal Principle is 'All Energy Moves Toward Balance.' Balance is the natural state of the universe—like a circle. A perfect circle is always in balance. The planet Earth is always in balance because of its opposite poles, and its balance between the sun and the other planets of your solar system. In electronics, there is a positive and a negative. In humans, there is a light side and a dark side. Both sides create balance. Balance, as in the example of the circle, enables all things to move toward an ultimate awareness, or their own perfection. Without balance, all things—including humans—lead a life of discord. With balance, there is perfection or Oneness, oneness with the Creator, God, the Divine Energy, the Universal Power—whichever term you choose."

Jonathan thought for a moment. He felt himself getting tired but wanted to finish this discussion. Ahmay was right: sometimes this stuff was pretty intense.

"I can see the logic of that," he said. "It's just like in music: without balance between different sections of an orchestra, there's less harmony, less counterpoint, less theme development, less perfection. Even within one instrument, say the piano for example, a composition would have less dimension if it were played mostly with one hand or within just one octave."

"Exactly," said Ramda. "Also the notion of good and bad promotes the concept of separateness, which leads to feelings of isolation and disconnection, which contradicts the principles we talked about earlier: 'Everything is Energy' and 'All Energy is Interconnected.' If everything is interconnected, then disconnection is impossible." Ramda paused. "Is this making sense to you?"

Jonathan nodded but couldn't get any words to come out. Suddenly, he was overcome with loneliness; he fought the urge to break into tears. The words "separateness" and "disconnection" and "isolation" rang over and over in his mind. That's you, Taylor, he thought to himself. Separate, disconnected, and isolated. You live by yourself, have no wife or girlfriend or children, go to work every day and bust butt and rarely ever talk to anyone. You hardly even know your neighbors. You're all alone, Taylor. You're Mr. Separateness. How did you let yourself get so screwed up?

I guess, he thought, it has a lot to do with how I was brought up. Well, that's not entirely true. Come on, you're beginning to sound like some of those people you used to counsel in Chicago—everything was someone else's fault. You can't blame your separateness on your parents or the Church or your education; you made the choices. It's true that much of the world is about separateness. It begins with "good" and "bad" and it goes from there: Satan versus St. Michael; Catholics versus Protestants; Christianity versus Atheism; Liberals versus Conservatives; North versus South; Totalitarianism versus Democracy; Freedom versus Slavery. But you, Taylor, you're the one who chooses to accept or reject or become a part of these concepts. No one else. It's just hard to admit you've spent so many of your 37 years being so "out of balance," so completely and utterly alone. So ... incomplete.

"Are you all right?" asked Ramda.

Jonathan nodded. "I think ... " He swallowed. "So energy just is," he said. "No 'good,' no 'bad'; just is. Sort of like emotions. I learned that back in my days as a therapist. Emotions are neither good nor bad; they just are. It's what we do about them that matters. Same with energy: everything is energy, it's all interconnected, and it just is. 'Good' and 'bad' are judgments, not energy. Energy can be out of balance, but that's an unnatural state because all things naturally seek their own perfection— their own highest and best use, as it were."

"Right again, Jonathan," Ramda said. "You are making real progress. Now, let us talk about the difference between separateness and Duality."

"What's Duality?"

"Duality is one aspect of reality," Ramda said, "a part of the Universal Principles; it exists whether it is perceived or not. Separateness is just a belief, often having more to do with focus than anything else. However, the concept of Duality is based on the premise that everything is present in all moments. If everything is energy and all energy is interconnected, then everything is One, and every part must contain the Whole.

"What that means," Ramda continued, "is that any moment you experience, anything you observe, anyone with whom you interact, contains its own whole or balance or perfection.

"If you believe your world to be separate, that self–fulfilling prophecy will seem to be true. Your world will taste, feel, and look separate, but it is an illusion. Duality says that everything is a part of the One; everything exists together at the same time."

Jonathan scowled. "So does that mean that what you see is not what you get; that there's really much more?"

"Remember when you and Ahmay discussed the idea of 'Your focus is your reality?'"

"Yes."

"That is the whole point," Ramda said. "Your reality is based upon your focus. Change your focus, and you change your reality. Have you ever tried that?"

Jonathan thought for a moment. "I think I have," he said. "I remember once I needed to buy a car, so I went to this place in San Diego called the 'Mile of Cars' that specializes in all kinds of different automobiles. One of the places offered a kind of car I'd never heard of: a Miada, a cute little sporty two–seat convertible. I told the salesman that I'd never seen this car before and he laughed. He told me it had been on the market for over a year, backed up by a multimillion-dollar ad campaign in newspapers and magazines as well as radio and TV. That puzzled me, until I drove home. On the way home I remember counting four Miadas. I guess I'd changed my focus."

"That is an accurate analogy about focus," said Ramda, "but here is the part that may be hard for you to accept about Duality: When you see something that you would call good—like someone who is helping out the community and who is idolized, remember that a dark side exists at that very moment as well. Conversely, when you turn on your television set and see the cruelty of an individual, know that there is also a warm and loving side to that person. That is Duality. It is a part of the concept of balance. Life is never an either/or but always a both/and. All energy is in balance; the challenge for you, Jonathan, is to change your focus and find, act, and feel the balance."

So how do I do that? Jonathan wondered. It'd be nice if some of this theorizing could help me resolve my audition problem.

"You will start to see the relevance very shortly," Ramda said. "Just stay with me a little longer. First, a couple of points.

"The question arises about what to do when something is out of balance, especially a human—say yourself. This conversation we're having began as a result of you saying that something you had not done was 'bad.' I suggested that it would be more accurate if you spoke of that behavior as being out of balance. So you may be asking yourself, what can I do to achieve balance? How do I do that?"

Jonathan shook his head and threw up his hands. "It'd be nice to have one private thought," he said good–

naturedly. "I feel like I'm standing here with no clothes on."

Ramda chuckled. "To me, you are."

"A computer with a sense of humor. This is really one for the book." Jonathan was silent for a moment. "Of course you're right. So, how do I correct my lack of balance?"

"By bringing the dark side into the light," Ramda replied. The computer screen flashed to life. Videos of the moon and Earth played side by side. Gradually, the camera moved in for a close-up on each one. "These two planetary bodies are perfect examples of this point. The moon's dark side never experiences the sun; it is separate and isolated. The result is a cold and desolate place where almost nothing can live. The Earth, on the other hand, rotates all its sides into the sun's light. The result is a nurturing and dynamic planet where there is much growth and abundance." The camera showed the differences between the two planetary surfaces. "You agree with that, Jonathan?"

"So how do I bring my dark side into the light?" he asked.

"By not believing that the dark side is separate; by learning from the dark side; but most of all, by talking about it," said Ramda. "By not being afraid to admit it exists, and why. That is how. Once it is there in the light of human discourse, it will not seem so powerful, so difficult to bring back into balance."

"Hmmm," Jonathan said. "I'll have to think about that one."

"The most important thing to remember is PEIS."

"You mean like piece of mind." said Jonathan jokingly.

"That too," Ramda said, "but more specifically the Physical, Emotional, Intellectual, and Spiritual. In humans, that is what needs to be in balance."

"How would you know? You're a computer. What would you know about the human condition?"

"Jonathan ... I am much more than a computer." He paused. "I can tell you this: At one time, I was human. I believe I know quite a lot about the human condition. But whether you believe me or not does not diminish the truth of my words. PEIS is where it is at—balance between all four aspects."

Jonathan sighed. "Sounds like enough work to keep me busy for the next couple minutes."

Ramda chuckled again.

The screen became blank and new words appeared: "Remember everyone is moving toward balance at his or her own pace. You have eternity. What is your rush?"

"Does that mean I can kick back and do nothing?"

"Sure, if that is your choice," Ramda answered. "Just bear in mind that everything is energy. Energy is always in motion—either toward balance or away from balance. In humans, it is either peace of mind or anxiety; you cannot experience both at the same time. If you decide to sit back too long and do nothing, you are probably going to be out of balance and therefore in great discomfort." He paused. "I know this bothers you, so I am reluctant to quote your own thoughts."

"Why break a perfect record, Ramda? You're on a roll."

"Did you not speak to yourself of an 'ache of discontent' after we had been talking about how, by an act of will, humans determine distribution of their total energies between the physical, emotional, intellectual, and spiritual energy centers?"

"That's right."

"So, you already know what I am talking about. The other side of that coin is that if you rush around like a chicken with its head cut off, trying to meet your own expectations, you are probably going to emphasize the intellect over the other energy centers. That will also cause imbalance."

Jonathan stretched and yawned. "I'm not bored, Ramda. Just on system overload. I think I need to take a break. But I've got one last question for you: Besides discussing and exploring my 'dark side' with others, what else should I do to bring myself back into balance?"

"Keep up the meditation and relax. When you get to where you are—frustrated from trying too hard—if you just ease up and cut yourself some slack, sometimes you will start moving toward balance and not even realize it. What happens is that you give yourself permission to hear your body, feel your emotions, and sense your intuition. To the outside world, it looks as though you are not doing anything, but you are really doing a lot. Writers, painters, and composers could not function without this. It is an essential part of the journey, and it is called 'letting go of thought.'"

Jonathan shook his head in confusion. "What?"

"Summarize what we have been talking about," said Ramda.

"Now?" asked Jonathan. For no apparent reason, he was suddenly feeling anxious, just like he did when he first came into the Celestial Bar. "I'm feeling a little overwhelmed by all this. Can we take a break?"

The room was silent. Jonathan noticed that Ahmay was gone.

"Sure," said Ramda. "I understand that there is a lot coming at you all at once." He chuckled. "Now you can go find Paula. That is really what is on your mind, is it not?"

Jonathan blushed and laughed at himself.

Chapter 8

"You cannot make a connection ... until you let go of your fear."

Jonathan stepped out of Ramda's beam of light into the empty Transition Room. He remembered that Ahmay said he might go out to the bar and talk with Zorinthalian. Jonathan was mentally drained from his session with Ramda, yet stark fear was quickly invading his thoughts. It was the same kind of panic that drove him into the Celestial Bar. He felt that his pursuer was close again and intended to hurt him—even kill him. Except there was no one else in the room.

"Hurry back," said Ramda. "I enjoyed our chat, but there is much more to cover."

"Yeah ... right," said Jonathan, heading for the sink. He needed something cold to drink. A snack or some fruit wouldn't hurt either. Maybe his blood sugar was running low and he was imagining things. How could there be a problem? He was in the Celestial Bar. No one could hurt him here, could they?

He opened cabinet doors, looking for a glass, and found a clean, empty jelly jar. He filled it with water, sat in one of the club chairs, and gulped. His hands were shaking so badly, he could barely keep from spilling.

Just then the door opened and in came the same barback who was behind the bar when Jonathan met Zorinthalian. He carried a rack full of clean water glasses.

He ignored Jonathan, stared at Ramda's light beam, and headed for the cabinets by the sink.

Jonathan sprang from his chair and moved quickly to the opposite side of the room, sliding in behind a couch. You'd better get ready, Taylor, he told himself, something nasty is about to develop here. "Ahmay!" he shouted out loud, "I need you in here now!" He scanned the room for something he could use to defend himself; he was sure the barback would attack at any moment.

The barback went about his business, occasionally taking a quick glimpse of the beam of light coming from the wall. He placed the clean glasses in the cabinet, picked up the empty rack, and was just opening the door to leave when Ahmay walked in. The two men walked around each other.

"Are you all right?" Ahmay asked Jonathan as he walked in and noticed him cowering in the corner.

Jonathan didn't answer. He was busy looking around the room, waiting for an unseen attacker to reveal himself. His fingers were almost white as he clutched the nearly empty jelly jar.

The barback was gone, and the feeling that something bad was about to happen diminished, but Jonathan still felt as though someone were after him. It can't be the barback, he told himself. Someone else is after me.

"What is the matter?" Ahmay asked. "Did something happen in here? You look like you are ready to fight."

"There's somebody in here," Jonathan said, voice trembling, darting his eyes side to side.

"What do you mean?" Ahmay wondered. He walked over beside Jonathan. "Did you see something?"

"I can feel him, it's just like when I first came into the bar. I knew he was there; I just couldn't see him."

"I see," Ahmay, nodded. He pushed his long black hair behind his ears. "How do you feel this very moment?"

"I feel better, but I know it's a trick. The minute you're gone, he's going to show himself. He's hiding in here somewhere as we speak."

"Well then, let us look for him."

The two men opened every cabinet, looked under and behind every piece of furniture, opened every closet door; there was no one.

Jonathan shook his head. "I must be losing my mind," he said. "You've got to believe me: there is someone in here. I've never been more sure of anything in my life. I can still feel his presence. I'm not imagining this, Ahmay."

"I believe you."

"I didn't call you in here on a wild goose chase."

Ahmay chuckled. "I know." He paused and smiled to himself while settling into one of the club chairs. "Actually, wild goose chases are rather fun, but ... that is another story. Because you were scared for your life, you called me back in here. That is what I asked you to do, and that is what you did. The question is, what do we do now?"

Jonathan took a chair beside him. For some reason, he was feeling more relaxed, less anxious. "Well, hopefully you'll be able to shed some light on this whole debacle. I know I have no clue, and there's no one else here, except Ramda."

Ahmay cleared his throat. "I think you need to talk with Ramda. This time I promise to stay here the whole time, but I think Ramda will help you the most. I know you are in a hurry and that is why I am recommending him."

Jonathan closed his eyes and shook his head. He then took a long, deep breath. "All right, all right. I'll talk to Ramda. You're a hard man, Ahmay. You asked me to trust you and I said I would. Ramda better have some answers, though; otherwise we're going to have to talk about this trust thing all over again."

"That seems fair," said Ahmay.

Without another word, Jonathan stood and walked back into the beam of light; it was still shining brightly from the wall.

"Ramda," said Jonathan, "I need your help."

The light beam flickered and there was a buzzing noise like electricity being shorted. Strange and discordant sounds came from the light beam.

"Calm down," advised Ahmay. "You cannot make a connection to Ramda until you calm down, until you let go of your fear. That will raise your VF."

Jonathan fought his emotions so he could focus. He knew Ahmay was right. Okay, okay, breathe, he thought. Remember Shawano Lake and fishing with Pop—that was a relaxing time. Okay, okay, I'm feeling better already.

"Welcome back," said Ramda. "That was quick."

"I've got a problem," Jonathan said. "I need your help."

"I know," said Ramda. "But first, let us go back to what I asked you to do just before you decided to take a break."

"You wanted me to summarize what we'd been talking about?"

"Correct."

Jonathan closed his eyes. As he had learned from meditating, he cleared his mind of all the anxiety and fear he had just experienced. Then he thought back to how he and Ramda had started with Divine Reality and his soul, followed by ... let's see—oh yes, Energy and Universal Principles. Next came Vibrational Frequencies (VF) and PEIS within all energy, especially humans; then Balance as the natural state of the universe, then ... what's next? Ah—the difference between separateness and Duality. Next came a repeat from Ahmay: your reality is your focus, and finally followed by ... let's see—oh, yeah ... the purpose to all this: everything is moving towards balance.

"Yes," said Jonathan, focusing on his thoughts with his eyes still closed, "I think I can recall most of what we discussed."

"You are right," Ramda said. "Open your eyes."

While Jonathan's eyes were closed, the computer monitor had returned and was now all lit up and blinking. Every thought he'd just had was displayed on the screen in big gold letters against a purple background. "Good grief, Ramda, couldn't you have given me a little warning? Is everything that I think from now on going to appear on this screen?"

Ramda chuckled. "No, Jonathan. I am just trying to make a point. What you see on the screen is a visual manifestation of another Law of Energy and that is, 'Energy Creates Form'—in this instance, thought."

"Great!" said Jonathan. "That clears up everything. I can't tell you how tickled I am that I asked. 'Thought Creates Form,' eh? Now I understand completely why I think someone's trying to kill me and that they're here in this room when they're not. Brilliant, Ramda. Just positively brilliant."

"Getting a little testy, Jonathan?"

"You might say that. I'm also getting sick and tired of asking questions and getting riddles instead of answers!"

"Well, did you ever stop and think that maybe you are getting the answers but that you are not understanding them? Or that when you do hear the answers, you do not take the trouble to adequately think them through? If the answers were easy to grasp, you would not need help now, would you?"

"Yes, that's true. I realize I may be the cause of all my own misunderstanding, but that realization doesn't help when my time here is so limited. I want to understand. I really do."

"Let us start with thought. Do you understand what I meant by 'Thought Creates Form'?"

"Not exactly. It sounds as if you're saying thoughts are energies that leave my body and eventually manifest themselves in the physical world."

"You are close," said Ramda. "Everything Is Energy including thoughts and, as you know, all Energy Has Vibrational Frequency or VF. Let us use a hypothetical example. Let us talk about violence in American society. It begins with ignorance: the notion that violence is an acceptable way to resolve conflict. That thought now has its own VF. That thought did not create nor destroy any energy, it merely gave the energy a new form—a new vibrational frequency.

"Now, two things happen to that thought, because all energy is interconnected. First, within the individual, this thought will now cause a redistribution of the PEIS energy systems; next, the individual will begin to behave in accordance with this thought. The thought will remain in a static condition until another thought either changes or contradicts it. So, to that extent, this new thought about violence being an acceptable behavior for conflict resolution remains within the individual. In other words, humans basically are what they think." Ramda paused. "With me so far?"

"So far so good," Jonathan replied.

"Thank you. The second thing that happens to this thought is that it will connect with the rest of the universe. Furthermore, because all energy has its own VF and tends to associate itself with energies of like VF, this reformatted energy will now re–associate itself with energies of like VF. This re–associative process becomes a further manifestation of the notion that Thought Creates Form." Ramda paused again. "Still with me?"

Jonathan nodded. "I'm still waiting to see how all this applies to me and my current problem with fear."

"We are almost there. Our hypothetical example is about violence being an acceptable solution to conflict. That thought is out of balance and will seek other out-of-balance energies of the same approximate VF. Eventually, this violent behavior between individuals will cause greater out-of-balance conditions. These thoughts will merge with others of like VF and become manifest in domestic violence, hate crimes, gang violence, civil conflicts such as in Ireland, Bosnia, and Rwanda, genocide, and finally regional and world wars."

Ramda paused while Jonathan absorbed these concepts.

"So, what thought produces," Ramda continued, "is a variation on a favorite American saying: What you think is what you get. Two simple examples come to mind from what you call movies: In 'Peter Pan,' Peter gets the kids to fly by convincing them that they can, and they do; in 'The Music Man,' professor Harold Hill gets the kids to play music by using 'the think system'—even though they have had no real music lessons, they think they can play their instruments, so they do.

"Jonathan, now do you see the connection to your situation?"

Jonathan took another long, deep breath. "I think so. You're saying that somehow the fear and panic that I was feeling just a few moments ago were caused by thought?"

"Correct."

"And since I know I didn't have any thoughts like that, those thoughts must have come from someone else. So the question must be, who thought those thoughts that caused me to feel as though my life was in so much danger? Is that right?"

"No, that is not it."

"Okay, so what is it?"

"You are going to have to supply the answer for yourself," said Ramda. "Remember, I am not your parent nor your protector. My job is not to save you from yourself; it is to show the way. In the final analysis, it is your journey."

"Why won't you answer my question?"

"I already have."

Jonathan began pacing the floor while still in the light, hands behind his back. "You already have, huh? I see I need to do some more thinking. Let me ask you one more question about thought. What about speech? If I have a thought and don't speak it, does it have the same impact as if I do?"

"Excellent question. Words have a tremendous impact upon the power of a particular thought. When you speak your thoughts, they are intensified because you are putting intellectual activity into physical form; the act of speech makes the thought all the more powerful. In your world, spoken or written thoughts can be somewhere in the area of a hundred times more powerful than unspoken or unwritten thoughts, in terms of how they impact form."

Jonathan kept pacing. "And that's true for out-of-balance as well as in-balance thoughts?"

"Precisely."

"Who decides if a thought is in balance or not?"

"No one. Either it is or it is not. No one decides."

Jonathan stopped pacing. "How are we humans supposed to understand?"

"You cannot understand it," said Ramda. "You can only know it by following the Universal Principles. If a thought promotes harmony, then it must be in balance; if a thought promotes disharmony, then it must be out of balance. Logically, as a musician, harmony is something that should be fairly easy for you to recognize. Are you comfortable with that?"

"Intellectually, I am," Jonathan said, rotating his neck and stretching to break his tension. There's too much going on at once, he thought. "I don't know how I'll feel when I have to try and figure out what's in or out of balance. But you've given me a lot to think about, and that's what I want to do right now: go think."

"Makes sense to me," said Ramda. "Do not forget: thinking is only part of the knowing process."

"Thanks for your help, Ramda. Sorry about getting testy."

"No problem. Come back any time."

Jonathan stepped out of the beam of light into the Transition Room. This time Ahmay was waiting, still dressed in faded jeans and seated in a club chair with his long legs crossed. He stared up at the ceiling. As Jonathan approached, the Native American looked him in the eye and grinned from ear to ear. "Well, young Bear, did you have an interesting journey with Ramda?"

Jonathan rolled his eyes. "Whew. I have to get out of here. I need fresh air and something to drink and some hot food. I feel like I've just climbed Mt. Everest!"

"Done," Ahmay chuckled. "Let us go see Zorinthalian; my treat. He will know exactly what to fix you."

Jonathan and Ahmay left the Transition Room and walked back up the corridor toward the bar. The smells of freshly cooked food and warm bread wafted into Jonathan's nostrils. His stomach growled. He remembered about Paula as they passed Conference Room 4. I wish I could talk to her right now, he thought. Someone less doctrinaire than Ahmay and Ramda would be a welcome relief; those two guys really put me through the meat grinder.

A forgotten thought began to bubble up in Jonathan's awareness. The problem is, I'm running out of time and stamina. Any minute, I may have to leave here and go back to that audition in Los Angeles. What I need is something to eat or drink that will give me the strength to concentrate and absorb all these "pearls of wisdom" I've been getting from Ramda and Ahmay. They mean well; I'm just running on empty. That's what happens, Taylor, when you don't eat regularly. How many times do you have to have it knocked into your head? If you don't take care of your body, how can you expect it to take care of you? Hope Zorinthalian has a few tricks up his sleeve. That reminds me: Maybe if I can get him talking, something will click and I'll remember where we've met before.

Ahmay took a seat at the bar and Jonathan joined him. He remembered that the last time he was at the bar, he'd experienced the same sense of danger he'd felt in the room with Ramda. Ramda's explanation—about thoughts creating form—didn't alleviate the fact that Jonathan was feeling that same fear again. He decided not to mention it this time.

"Gentlemen?" said Zorinthalian, standing in front of them, waiting for their order. "You drinking or eating or both?"

"Both," blurted Ahmay. "Young Bear, here," he said, jerking a big rugged thumb at Jonathan, "will have a glass of the house draft and a menu. I will have some more of that moon tea, only this time, I want it boiling hot. My last cup was so cold I thought it was iced tea without the cubes."

The words were no sooner out of his mouth than the beer, tea, and menu were on the bar in front of Jonathan and Ahmay.

"How did you do that?" wondered Jonathan, taking a long swig of his beer. "That's the fastest service I've ever seen and I've been a bartender, for Pete's sake."

The tall man behind the counter smiled kindly and looked Jonathan in the eye. The visitor from San Diego felt a tingling sensation throughout his body; his anxiety level was falling. "Practice," said Zorinthalian, going about his work while still looking Jonathan in the eye. "It is nothing more than practice."

Ahmay sipped his tea and checked the menu. "You know, Zorinthalian, everything on here looks so good, I don't know what to order. Just bring me something?"

The bartender nodded at Ahmay and turned to Jonathan. "How about you: ready to order?"

For reasons he couldn't grasp, Jonathan felt much better, and he downed the rest of his beer. "I'll have another one of these and ... you can order for me, too. Whatever this house draft is, it's the best-tasting beer I've ever had."

The second beer appeared almost as if by magic, and Jonathan couldn't get over how quickly his whole attitude had changed. Zorinthalian, having set out their silverware, went to wait on other customers.

"Well, what do think, young Bear," asked Ahmay, grinning like a Cheshire cat, "you going to live?"

Jonathan nodded vigorously. "I can't believe how much better I feel. For a minute there, I actually felt like there was no way I could digest all that stuff you and Ramda had been telling me; I felt like I'd been hit by a runaway freight train. I was almost ready to give up."

Ahmay's smile vanished and his face becomes serious. "Well, we did cover a lot of material, but you can handle it. Of that I am sure. Whenever you feel overwhelmed, it is usually a good time to go back to basics: The Universal Principles. You can never go wrong with them, and there is always something new to be learned from them."

Jonathan nodded. "Like the interconnectedness of all energy."

"Right. And what does that one concept say to you about all these new ideas Ramda and I have been throwing at you?"

Jonathan raised his eyebrows and sipped on his beer. "To broaden my focus, allow for new perspectives. With that comes more balance and harmony, and then, even more balance." He paused. "The one thing that sticks out in my memory is something Ramda said, 'Everyone is moving toward balance at their own pace. You have eternity. What's your rush?'"

Ahmay chuckled. "Right. As they say on Earth, you need to 'lighten up, dude.' You are going to get it. There is no doubt in my mind. Just let it flow, dude; I mean, like, it is totally rad."

Jonathan laughed. "I don't know if I'm ready for a wise–cracking computer and a Valley–talking Shoshone, all on the same day."

"That is Shoshone chief to you, paleface."

Both men broke out in hearty laughter.

Zorinthalian arrived with plates of hot food. "If you do not like this, Jonathan, let me know. It will be a new taste for you, but I think you will like it. It will help you feel better, too." He left.

Jonathan sampled the food; it was delicious. "Mmmmm. This is great," he said, swallowing another mouthful while thinking about Zorinthalian's words. He hadn't told Zorinthalian that he wasn't feeling well.

"Good grief, Jonathan," Ahmay said between bites, "how many times do we have to read your mind before you are going to get it? All of the staff here are telepathic. That is why we get the big bucks."

Again, both men roared.

Man, it doesn't get any better than this, Jonathan thought. Good food, good drink, and a friend to share a laugh with. It's been a long time since you had a male friend with whom you could share a good belly-laugh, Taylor. It's weird, though; there's something unusually familiar about this room and this place. I feel as if I've been here before and yet nothing quite comes back into focus.

He looked around the bar at the other customers.

Look at all those people; there are so many of them. They look at me as if they know me, and it feels as if I know them, too, but not one of their names comes to mind. Still, sitting here laughing and joking with Ahmay and Zorinthalian feels more like family and friends than anything I've felt in a long, long time. The only thing that would make it more perfect is if Paula were here.

Jonathan looked over at Ahmay. He was sipping his moon tea. Jonathan noticed a warming sensation in the middle of his back. The hot spot worked its way through his body to the area of his heart. As the warmth increased in intensity, he realized the feeling was not going to go away. He spun on the bar stool to investigate. It was Paula. She was standing right behind him.

He felt his heart jump. Her stunning beauty took his breath away. There she stood, with her blonde hair tucked up in a tight bun, her big brown eyes almost even with his. They seemed to be pleading with him about something. He recalled her words about needing to speak with him at the end of her shift and then the images flashed across his consciousness again. He saw them together in other times and places, holding hands and kissing and naked and laughing and staring into each other's eyes.

She turned to Ahmay. "I know what you are going to say, but I need to talk with Jonathan for just a quick minute."

Ahmay gave her a long glare and got up. He gave Jonathan a quick glance, a faint smile playing in one corner of his mouth, and started to leave. He turned back to Jonathan. "We still have much to discuss. When you are done, Zorinthalian will know where to find me." He left.

As Ahmay walked away, Paula took Jonathan's hand and led him toward an empty booth. As they walked, he again noticed the grand piano; it seemed lonely there, sitting by itself in a corner. All the booths were full of people laughing and talking and eating, but no one appeared interested in that piano. Finally Paula found an empty booth. She slid in and pulled him in beside her. Their knees touched. Their eyes locked and she took both his hands in hers. He could feel her gentle, strong fingers softly caressing his palms.

Her brown eyes were swimming with emotion as they bore in on him, probing deep inside, to the depths of his soul. He felt his heart doing flip–flops. For a split second, he felt as if he were back in high school in south Chicago.

"You still do not remember who I am, do you?" she whispered.

He shook his head no. "I'm trying real hard," he said, his heart singing with joy to be in her very presence. He felt like he wanted to sing. He couldn't imagine being any happier. "It's like I've dreamed about you but can't recall the dream."

"We have visited in your dreams," she said. "And we did meet many times in life. What I am about to tell you will not make much sense, but I want you to let me go. You have been holding on to my memory in your present life for too long and that act has been holding you back from moving into meaningful relationships."

Jonathan frowned. His heart sunk with fear and disbelief. "What are you talking about? I just found you and you're telling me to forget you? Fat chance."

"Part of you remembers me," she continued. "It is that part that worries me. It keeps looking for me in your world and I am not there—at least not in the form you wish. This misdirected focus is causing you to block your heart to others who want to love you."

Jonathan smiled. "Paula, you're not making any sense."

Her eyes got bigger and she looked scared. "You know my name. You remember quite a bit, do you not?"

"Yes, but not from my head, from my heart," he said, "and I know I love you."

"Holding onto that thought is causing imbalance within you," she blurted. "It is better if you let go."

"Oh, stop all this foolish talk!" He took one of her hands. "Come here, I want to show you something."

He slid out of the booth, pulling her with him. They headed for the piano. Suddenly, an electricity of excitement swept through the crowd in the booths and tables. "All right, Jonathan!" shouted someone as the couple neared the piano.

"What are you doing?" Paula said, "I am going to get in so much trouble. I am supposed to be working."

"Relax," he said. "You're with me. This will just take a minute. You'll like it. I'm dedicating it to you."

She started to speak, but stopped and let go of his hand. She cocked her head to one side and took a deep breath as he slid onto the piano stool. Her big, brown eyes were filling with tears.

He blew on his hands and rubbed them together, got comfortable, and began to play the first movement from his concerto. Now he could feel the emotion coursing through his veins, filling his very being. This is why you wrote this piece, he reminded himself. Let it flow. Let the energy flow.

He closed his eyes. That's it. Nice and gentle and slow at the beginning. There's no hurry. You've got a whole concerto to work with here. Take your time. Remember, no one has the music, only you. You can improvise all over the place if you want. Oh, this feels so right. It's the best you've ever played it.

He thought of Paula's beautiful face and her tears and her concern for his happiness. He felt like he wanted to cry with joy for having found her love, but he played on. He wanted to hold her and tell her he loved her for endless moments, days, and years, yet he knew she must leave his company and go back to work until who knew when. And he played on.

Then he remembered Ahmay and Ramda and Zorinthalian and the bizarre incident in the Transition Room. He felt as though he wanted to pick up the tempo, and he played on. He couldn't believe how much information and new ideas had been thrown at him since he'd arrived. He played faster now. Where is all this going? I can't get any fix on time here. Why do I feel as if I should be in such a hurry? Oh yeah ... L.A. Boy, Digger, the longer you're here, the harder it is to remember your life back in Southern California. Actually, I'm running out of time. The people ahead of him at the audition must not have that much more to go, and that meant he would have to leave this place and be separated from Paula.

The thought sent chills through his soul, and he slowed his playing. Being unable to see her and be with her caused a sadness to invade his heart. Now he would have to fight the loneliness and rejection if, when he stopped playing, she was gone. He shouldn't have forced this on her. All he was thinking about was himself. Not much balance there, Taylor. He swallowed a smile at the thought of Ahmay and his crazy ways. The movement ended; he stopped playing. He opened his eyes.

Paula was still standing there beside the piano, tears running down her cheeks. Thunderous applause erupted from the restaurant and bar. "Way to go, Jonathan," yelled one excited patron, "where the hell you been, boy?"

Paula touched his hands while the crowd was still cheering. That familiar piercing warmth filled his hands and fingers. "That was beautiful," she said. "Thank you.

You have a great talent. But I have to go. Remember what I said: You need to let me go."

"And you remember what I said," he answered.

"I will see you again before you leave. Things will be clearer for you then." She turned to leave.

"Don't go," he said, reaching for her hands. He felt the pain in his heart and it was almost more than he could bear. "Please don't leave now. I haven't finished."

The crowd was standing and cheering now.

She stopped and came back close to him. "Jonathan, please do not make this any harder for either of us." Tears were still streaming down her face. He felt the wetness on his own cheeks. "We have met many times before." She wiped the tears from his face and kissed him softly on the lips. "I love you with all my heart, but it is better for you if you release me. We will talk more of this later." She kissed him again. "Now finish your piece." She nodded and smiled at the applauding crowd, then turned back to Jonathan. "Your public awaits, and I want to hear how you handle that second movement. I understand that sometimes it can be a little problem."

She winked and strolled back toward the conference rooms.

Chapter 9

"What the (world) really needs ... is more servers"

As Jonathan stood beside the piano, watching Paula disappear down the corridor toward the conference rooms, an emptiness crept into his heart. With two quick swipes he cleared the tears from his cheeks. What was sheer delight and joy just seconds before had become a hollow aching that he thought would not end until he and Paula were together again. The applause of the dining and drinking guests continued, but he barely heard them. "Encore, encore!" they shouted. Jonathan raised a hand. The crowd became quiet.

He cleared his throat and swallowed. "Thank you for your kind applause," he said, looking around the room at their eager faces. "I realize many of you know me and that I've been gone from this place for some time. What I just played was the first movement of a work–in–progress that, as you can plainly hear, still needs more ... work."

"Play all of it," yelled someone from the crowd. "It sounds great to me."

"I agree," said another and everyone clapped.

Jonathan held up his hand again. "That's very kind of you, all of you," he said, looking around. "Right now I need to go finish the meal my hosts have provided. My young body here ... " He patted his soft midsection and everyone laughed. "As you can see, my poor body here needs some healthful sustenance." He took a deep breath.

"After that, I have several more appointments and then, if there's time, I'll come back to this beautiful piano and play the rest of the piece. Meantime, I'd like to thank all of you for making me feel so welcome and being so supportive at a time when I really need it." He nodded at several in the crowd who waved as if they knew him very well. "Thanks again," he said and headed for the bar.

The room exploded with applause and cheers. As he reached the bar, a few of the customers came up and shook his hand. Jonathan acknowledged their remarks with a word of thanks for each. Finally, the commotion stopped and he was left to finish his meal.

Just as he lifted his fork to begin eating, Zorinthalian cleared away the old dishes and replaced them with fresh, hot servings of the same food. The muscular bartender looked Jonathan in the eye and raised his eyebrows. "Nice playing, but if you are going to eat, it might as well be fresh and hot, right? Nothing worse than cold hot food."

Jonathan nodded agreement. "Thanks," he said, beginning to eat. "That was very thoughtful of you."

He took a few more bites and considered the rushing images—now flashing through his mind—of past brotherhood and joy that he had experienced with Zorinthalian in ancient times. Surely, this mountain of a man knew what was going through his mind and yet did not speak of it. There must be a reason. Jonathan decided to let it be for the moment.

"You know," he continued, "I've been watching you. I don't mind saying, you're the best bartender I've ever seen."

Zorinthalian smiled while cleaning off the bar. "Thank you, Jonathan. Coming from a man of your judgment, knowledge, and experience, I consider that a real compliment."

"You're welcome," Jonathan said. I guess that was his way of saying I did right, he thought. "I'm sure you're just like me, though: whenever you sit at a bar, you automatically start running your checklist."

Zorinthalian looked confused. "What checklist?"

"You know," Jonathan said, "checking out bartenders: how they present themselves to the customer; their eye contact; how much they talk; what they say; do they check with the customer too much or too little; how they handle complaints; is their primary concern the customer's satisfaction or their tip; how they handle small tips; do they anticipate the customer's needs; their promptness in removing dishes and glasses; their knowledge of food and beverage.

"It's almost compulsive with me," he continued. "Anyway, you scored higher than anyone I've ever checked, even me."

Zorinthalian chuckled while rearranging things under the bar. "How do you like the restaurant business after all these years?" he asked. "How do you keep a fresh attitude?"

Jonathan shrugged and sipped his beer. "I suppose it's the people who keep me going," he said. "Sometimes at work or during a ball game, some of the guys will shoot the bull. Usually I just listen. People let their hair down, and it doesn't take long to find out that we're all pretty much coming from the same place. None of us expect to spend the rest of our lives in the restaurant business; it's just a stepping stone. The question everyone wrestles with is, what's the next step? That question is kind of what keeps us looking out for each other. We feel this inexplicable connection but can't find its purpose."

The bartender stopped working and studied Jonathan's face. "Maybe that is something you can find out while you are here. Maybe your next step is not so much a what, but a how."

A couple signaled for Zorinthalian. "Drinks all around," they said, "we want to make a toast." In a flash, Zorinthalian filled wine glasses in front of everyone at the bar. "We want to toast to our new journey," said the woman. "May we learn our lessons well."

"Here, here," said everyone, clinking their glasses.

Zorinthalian stopped in front of Jonathan. "By the way," he said, "as a student of the profession, do you know how the custom of clinking glasses during a toast started?"

"No, not really, but I'll tell you an answer I heard given once," Jonathan chuckled. "Back in medieval days, noblemen often tried to kill each other by poisoning each other's drinks. So when they clanked their goblets together and the wine spilled from one goblet to the other, it was an insurance policy."

Zorinthalian roared with laughter. "Only on Earth could one hear such an outrageous story! Let me tell you what I heard. Some perceptive server noticed that when making a toast, all the senses were being used except one: they could see the color of the wine, smell the bouquet, feel the wine as it passed the lips, and taste as the wine was sipped. But there was no sound—one sense had been omitted from the process. There could be no balance in the enjoyment of the wine until sound was added. Ergo, clanking goblets or clinking glasses."

Jonathan smiled. "Proof positive that the planet Earth needs more bartenders: so we can make sure everyone has a glass during a toast. That way, we're helping promote balance, and nobody can deny that the Earth needs more balance."

"What the planet Earth really needs," said Zorinthalian, "is more servers. The social workers, day care providers, teachers, nurses, volunteers, front line employees, bartenders, waiters, waitresses, and many other professions are truly servers. People who are in the service field are a dying breed, especially on your Earth. Look at those who are compensated the most; they are not servers. Your society seems to place more value on finding physical balance. Intellectual, emotional, and spiritual balance come in a poor second. That in itself is an out-of-balance condition which, if allowed to continue, will lead to more lack of balance."

"Will that ever change?" asked Jonathan.

"It is happening right now. To start with, there is an increase in the number of people designing lives of service, and business here at the Celestial Bar is getting better all the time. More people like you are making visits in the middle of their journey."

Zorinthalian leaned over. "One last thing, Jonathan, about the qualifications of a good server: they need to have a great memory. They need to remember who they are, what they are doing, and why they are doing it. And then, act on it."

The bartender left to help the barback unload a tray of glasses at the other end of the bar.

It was clear to Jonathan that Zorinthalian had no intention, at the moment, of trying to clear up the mystery about how they had known each other in another time and place. Just be patient, Jonathan kept telling himself; there's no real rush about these things.

Besides, that sense of impending danger he'd had in the Transition Room was returning. He looked around. Nothing had changed. Zorinthalian and the same barback were behind the bar; there were no new customers at the bar or in the restaurant; there was no one close to him who looked suspicious or threatening. He gulped down his beer.

Ahmay slid onto the bar stool beside him. "Well, well," he said, "it is about time you got serious about taking care of your body."

Jonathan smiled and glanced over at Ahmay. "This food and drink are wonderful. I can't believe the difference they've made; I feel like a new man."

"Maybe you are, young Bear," said Ahmay. "Maybe you are. Are you ready to continue your journey?"

"Absolutely," Jonathan said, nodding his head with vigor, "but there's one thing I want to ask you before that."

Ahmay turned and looked into his guest's eyes. "Okay."

"Do you know why I keep getting these powerful feelings of danger? I'm getting one right now and it's driving me nuts."

"Yes, I know."

Jonathan stared into the Native American's eyes and cold chills covered his body; he wasn't sure if he wanted to ask the next question. "Will you tell me why, right now?"

Ahmay motioned for Zorinthalian to join them. "Jonathan has a question," he said to the bartender. "He is asking if I know why he is having these ongoing feelings of imminent danger. I told him I did. Now he wants me to explain myself. What do you think?"

Zorinthalian shrugged. "Yeah, I think he is ready."

"You mean you both know?" Jonathan blurted.

Both men nodded.

"Well, will one of you please hurry up and tell me before I lose my mind?"

"Sure," said Zorinthalian. "It is the barback. He is the one who appears to be after you. He is the same guy who chased you in here."

"But he doesn't look anything like the guy who chased me in here. How can it be the same guy?"

Both men chuckled. "He can change his appearance any time he wants," said Ahmay. "It does not change who he is."

"Well, who is he?"

"For you, Jonathan, it is not so much a question of who but what," said Ahmay, "and that is a question we cannot answer. That one you are going to have to figure out for yourself."

There was a long silence while Jonathan studied both their faces, trying to decide what to do next. "You guys are serious?"

They both nodded.

"Bartender," one of the other customers yelled.

"Whistle if you need me," Zorinthalian said as he left.

Jonathan's head was spinning.

"It is not that big of a deal, young Bear. You are safe here as long as you are with one of us. He just likes to scare the stuffings out of people. He is really past his prime. No one in here pays much attention to him."

Jonathan shook his head, trying to make sure he was hearing correctly. "So this is routine stuff for you folks?"

"That is right," Ahmay nodded. "Those kinds of guys are a dime a dozen in here. They come and they go. The staff here doesn't pay them much mind. They keep thinking they will catch one of us with our guard down. It has never happened. It is the visitors who are scared."

Jonathan frowned, trying to make sense of all this. They told you to relax, Taylor, and you just wouldn't leave it alone, would you? The whole time you've been in here, you've been scared to death for no apparent reason. No reason at all! It's the stupid barback, dummy! Un–freaking–believable. To be honest, Jonathan thought, this new revelation was a little bit anticlimactic.

"A little disappointed?" Ahmay chimed in.

"No. Not at all," Jonathan protested. "Why would I be disappointed?"

"Well, all drama junkies really get into crises," Ahmay said with a wink.

"I'm not a drama jun ... " He thought of Chicago and the Keys.

"Jonathan," Ahmay jumped in, "lately you are doing much better. Slowly but surely you are learning that you do not have to create a major upset in your life to make a change. But you still needed a little adrenaline rush to get you into the Celestial Bar."

Jonathan just stood there. There was no escaping the facts of his life. Just thinking about them made him feel a little embarrassed.

"Just a little advice, though, about guys like the barback. When one of those guys gets turned loose in the physical world, watch out. They can really do some damage; they have no self–control. Their only motivation is self–preservation.

"So," Ahmay added as casually as if they'd just been discussing the weather, "now that we have that out of the way, are you ready to continue your journey?"

Feeling like he'd just been hit between the eyes with a sledgehammer, Jonathan turned to Ahmay and nodded, barely.

"Good. Bring your drink. There is someone I want you to meet. He is a nice guy—a bit reserved for my taste, but you will like him. He really knows his beans."

The tall Shoshone chief stood and walked toward the booth area. Jonathan followed, feeling a small sense of relief.

The barback finished cleaning behind the bar and glanced over at Jonathan's table. He hummed an Irish ballad.

Ahmay slid into a booth beside a small, balding, elderly man with horned–rim glasses, a coat, and a bow tie. "Jonathan, I would like to have you meet an associate of mine. This is Mark."

They shook hands.

"How do you do?" Mark said. His voice was high and nasal, his hands small, strong, and soft.

"Just fine," Jonathan answered. "Nice to meet you, Mark. Any friend of Ahmay's can't be all bad."

The three men smiled.

"Mark has some information I think will help you, Jonathan. I have asked him to speak with you for a few minutes before you go back. I am going back to the bar. If you need me, just call." He slid out of the booth and stood. "Any problems?"

"Do I have to go back, even if I don't want to?" Jonathan blurted out, talking from his heart. "The scenery here is more beautiful than I remembered."

Ahmay knew Jonathan was talking about not wanting to leave Paula behind. "That is your choice," he said, trying to be casual. "Your decision to visit here was for just that: a visit, not a permanent stay. In fact, it was for a new beginning back there." He paused and studied Jonathan's face. "You do not have to think about that now. For the present, Mark has some pointers about how you can bring more balance into your entire body." Ahmay left.

Jonathan turned to Mark. "How can you do that?"

"I am a doctor," said the small man, adjusting his glasses.

"And what kind of a doctor are you?" asked Jonathan, feeling an immediate dislike for this man.

His knee–jerk reaction to doctors had always been one of mistrust, going back to childhood. He'd watched how their family doctors mistreated his parents' illnesses; they seemed more interested in prescribing drugs than in discovering the root causes for his parents' symptoms. He'd witnessed the same phenomenon in his own adult life, both in Chicago and in Florida. This guy's probably just like those other clowns, he thought.

Mark rubbed his neck. "Well, being a doctor here at the Celestial Bar is different than most doctors you have been familiar with. Here, my role is more of a healer than a technician or scientist; here we treat the whole person."

Jonathan was having a hard time being civil to Mark. He was trying to find some acceptable social expression for the repressed anger from his days with doctors who mis–diagnosed so many of his illnesses, some even ending in unnecessary operations.

"The whole person, eh, and how do you do that?"

"You do not like me very much do you, Jonathan? In fact, it is all you can do to be civil to me."

Jonathan blushed. "Yes, sir," he said, looking the doctor straight in the eye, "that's exactly correct."

"I do not blame you, given your family's and your personal medical history. The medical profession on Earth has gotten away from its original purpose—out of balance, if you will. But at this moment there is an opportunity for great change: alternative medicine has recently challenged Western medical doctrines. However, when Western doctors come to see alternative medicine as complementary medicine, that will be when they become healers with balance. My hope is that you will give me a chance to prove that I am a healer with balance. If I fail, then at least I will know you heard me out."

"That would be more fair, wouldn't it?" Jonathan agreed.

"Thanks," Mark said. "The first thing I want to mention in connection with your body is something you have already heard: Energy Must Flow Freely. Remember that?"

"Right," said Jonathan. "Ahmay and Ramda and I have been talking quite a bit about that. It falls under one of the Universal Principles."

Mark signaled for a waitress. "Want a refill?"

"Yes. Does wonders for my stamina."

The waitress took their order and left.

"The subject of health," Mark explained, "can be understood as an energy package; it is a combination of many different kinds of energy. They range from individual cells to organs to the complex systems such as the nervous or circulatory systems. For the body to be operating in 'good health,' the whole body needs to be in harmony with itself or 'in balance.' Make sense?"

Jonathan nodded.

"Another Law of Energy that is important for a better understanding of health is: All Energy Has Vibrational Frequency or VF. When cells or organs are in balance, they resonate within a certain frequency range; that range is what is considered 'healthy.' When the cell moves out of balance, the VF begins to lower—the energy moves slower and becomes more dense, like water when it becomes ice. This lower VF generally signals an 'unhealthy condition.' Since Energy Is Interconnected, all of the various cells and organs rely on each other for balance."

Jonathan smiled. "It's amazing how all aspects of humankind are so interrelated. So much of what you just mentioned, I've already discussed with Ramda and Ahmay, but within an entirely different framework."

"I understand," said Mark, "and you are absolutely right. That is why I mentioned earlier that, here, we treat the whole person."

The waitress returned with their drinks. "Thanks," he said. "Keep the drinks coming, all right?"

She smiled. "Yes, sir."

After she left, Mark shrugged, "The beer cannot hurt us. What they call beer here is nothing more than special fruit juices and herbs doctored up to look and taste like beer. There is no alcohol served here, period."

Jonathan chuckled and shook his head. "Good grief, this place is just full of surprises. Beer that isn't beer. What next?"

Mark reached inside his suit jacket and pulled out a note pad and pen. "I want to make a little sketch for you. I think it will help you understand how the body works." He drew what looked like a car radio with a giant antenna. "You understand the principle of how radios work on Earth, right?"

"Yes."

"And you understand the principle of radio waves with different wave lengths?"

Jonathan nodded.

"Well," continued Mark, "the human body is much like a radio that can receive all radio waves at once. In this analogy, there are only four radio waves. One of the functions of the mind is to act as the tuner which decides which of the waves it will receive."

Mark made four sets of up and down wavy lines passing through the radio's antenna. "The tightest and highest frequency wave lengths represent the highest vibrational frequency in the human body: spirituality. The next highest is the emotional, then the intellect; the lowest and thickest wave lengths represent the physical aspects of the human body." Mark turned the drawing around for Jonathan to look at. "You with me?"

"Got it."

"Now," Mark said, turning the drawing back toward himself and sketching another line under each wavy line, "this spirituality radio wave—as it were—has one unusual characteristic: it is bifurcated; the others are not. One half of the spirituality radio wave permeates and improves the other three radio waves. The quality of the reception is then either enhanced or impeded by the level of resistance of the internal wiring. The other part of the spirituality radio wave simply exists as its own broadcast from the source.

"In other words, the spirit or the soul, however you wish to characterize it, is a combination of all aspects of the four energy systems—PEIS—physical, emotional, intellectual, and spiritual. I realize you have already talked at length about PEIS with the others, so I will not waste your time trying to explain that."

"Now I get it," Jonathan said. "I remember when I first entered Ramda's light field, there were colors flowing from various parts of my body; other parts of my body had no colors whatsoever. Ramda said that the colors represented the flow of my soul or spirit through my body. So where there were no colors, there must have been an impediment or blockage."

"Exactly," said Mark. "Those portions of your body are out-of-balance. Following our analogy of the radio, there is either no reception of the radio waves or there is a short someplace. And, too often, these blockages or out-of-balance conditions began as unresolved spiritual issues and have worked their way down through the intellectual and emotional to the physical. That is what pain and discomfort are: blocked energy."

"I'm with you so far, Doc," Jonathan said playfully.

Mark adjusted his bow tie and suppressed a smile. "Maintaining these blockages, requires much more energy—something like ten times more—than just letting them go. That is how we heal ourselves: we let go, in our spirit, mind, heart, and body. It can begin with a thought—an act of will, if you please—and becomes a self–fulfilling prophecy: I believe I will heal, therefore I do. You and Ramda talked about this, remember; Thought Creates Form."

"So all I need to do is think healing?"

"No, that is not all," said Mark. "You would never try to think a broken leg healed; you would call a doctor. But if you were thinking 'healthy' thoughts before the accident, you might have lessened the damage. And if you create 'healing' thoughts after the mishap, you can accelerate the healing process.

Alternative and Western medicine have the potential to be complementary. It is an integrated process. Whenever you heal any part of yourself, the other parts will begin to be healed as an extension of the principle of interconnectedness. When the mind is fully at peace, so will the body be at peace with itself. When the heart knows love in all things, so will the spirit, mind, and body. When the body is in balance, the others rejoice with it. Humans are one of the most apt examples in all creation of synergism at work."

Jonathan scratched his head. "So how can I get my physicalness together?"

Mark adjusted his glasses. "Listen to your body; it knows what it needs."

"Is that all?"

"No," said Mark. "You can also do it by raising your VF's: eat healthfully and exercise. Both raise vibrational frequencies."

"I can see it all now," Jonathan said. "By 1998 on Earth, the commercials on Saturday mornings will sound something like"—he changed his voice to that of a make–believe announcer— "'Remember, boys and girls, Crunchy Munchie Cereal contains 600% higher VF's than brand X. Be a winner, have the highest VF on your block, eat Crunchy Munchies.'"

Mark smiled.

"You smiled. I knew you could do it, Doc."

"Actually," Mark said, recovering his composure, "that's probably not too far from the way things will be. Sooner or later, the mass consciousness of humans is going to discover VF's, and when they do, it will revolutionize health care on Earth. The higher the body's vibrational frequencies, the more energy can move through your body and the stronger the immune system can become. With a stronger immune system comes less illness or disease."

Jonathan took a deep breath and sipped his beer before asking his next question. "You're not suggesting, are you Doc, that if we humans were to follow all your suggestions that we could virtually eliminate sickness and disease from the planet Earth?"

"Let's just stick with you. I am saying that such a scenario is possible on an individual basis."

"What does that mean?"

"Health," Mark said, sipping his beer, "is about choices and energy and interconnectedness. If your focus is on those concepts, then being in balance will flow as a natural result. If you believe that sickness is something you get from someone or somewhere else, your focus is on separateness, which denies and ignores the Universal Principles. These are choices. Now if you do not understand or cannot accept the Universal Principles, then you may choose—choose in a cosmic sense—to learn more about life and the Universal Principles by allowing sickness into your life.

"Let us talk about pain; it is a gift. Pain is the body's way of saying it is not in balance."

Jonathan frowned. "You don't really expect anyone on Earth to believe that pain is a gift, do you?"

"No," said Mark. "No one will ever understand pain if they focus only on their physical existence. In order to fully comprehend the notion of pain, one must also see themselves from a spiritual perspective, simultaneous with their physical focus.

"Again, you may not be making a choice to create pain on a conscious level, but the fact is you are in charge of what you do, on a spiritual or soul level. No one else is. Remember, we are all seeking balance at our own pace. We have all eternity. There is no rush."

Jonathan looked puzzled. "So you're saying that sickness and disease can only come into our lives if we permit—on some level—out-of-balance conditions to exist within ourselves—our PEIS? It's the out-of-balance condition that produces a lack of healthfulness; sickness and disease are not responsible, we are?"

"Precisely," Mark said. "That is not to trivialize the tragic results of sickness or disease. Quite the contrary. The manifestation of lack of balance within any human is indeed something that requires compassion, understanding, and love by all fellow humans. But that is something for you to more fully explore with Ahmay or Ramda. My job is to make you aware of how healthfulness interconnects and interacts within the human body, mind, heart, and spirit. My hope is that my explanations about all these things will in some small way aid in your journey." He paused to clear his throat. "How am I doing?"

"Pretty darn well, I'd say," Jonathan said. As he finished his beer, he noticed the bump that was on his little finger. It took a moment for his memory to click in; then he remembered about his audition. "One final question, Doc. Are you saying that my injured right finger is the product of an energy blockage, and that I have it within my power to remove that blockage and bring myself into a more balanced condition?"

"That is exactly what I am saying. No more, no less. You have that ability, right now. I am not making any promises that you will, and it is not my job in this moment to show you how. I am simply saying that you have that power."

Maybe that's it, Jonathan thought to himself. Maybe that's why all this is happening. Maybe I can cure that finger before the time for my audition comes. "So who can help me?" Jonathan asked. "I want to work on that problem right away. My audition will be coming up any time now."

Mark studied Jonathan for a moment. "I think you had better go talk to Ahmay."

Chapter 10

" ... you are in charge ... "

Jonathan slid from the booth, stood, and shook hands with Mark. "Thanks," he said. "You've been a big help."

"Thank you," Mark said, adjusting his glasses and bow tie. "Just remember, Jonathan, you have the power within you to accomplish much. Your challenge will be to focus on that power and then learn to use it."

"I hear you, Doc. And that's what I fully intend to do." He turned to leave, stopped, and turned for one last look at the short man. "Thanks again," he said, with a self-conscious wave. "You've really opened my eyes." Then he whirled and hurried off.

He knew what he had to do. Arriving at the bar, he asked Zorinthalian, "Do you know where Ahmay is? I need to see him right away."

He spotted the barback working in the rear of the bar, stocking the beer cooler. A flash of fear shot across Jonathan's mind, and he shook his head. No you don't, Taylor, he told himself. Forget that crap. You've got more important things to think about right now.

Zorinthalian's face took on a strange expression.

"Right here, young Bear," Ahmay said from behind him.

Jonathan turned. "Where'd you come from?"

Ahmay smiled good-naturedly. "You went right by me."

"Can we talk … in private … right now?"

Ahmay shrugged. "Sure. What have you got in mind?"

"Let's go back to the Transition Room," Jonathan said, picking up the fresh "beer" Zorinthalian set out on the bar. "Thanks," he nodded at the bartender. Turning back to Ahmay, he continued, "We won't be disturbed there, and I've got some serious questions to ask you and Ramda. I need answers right away before my time here runs out."

"Let us go," said Ahmay, walking toward the corridor. "If you are waiting on me, you are backing up."

Minutes later, Jonathan closed the door to Transition Room 6 and took a deep breath. Ahmay was already sitting in one of the club chairs, legs crossed, sipping on a canned drink. The beam of light was still shining from a small opening in one wall, spreading out into a huge circle near the opposite wall. The special video and sound equipment center appeared to have been left undisturbed; small green and red lights blinked beside the "On" and "Off" switches.

Jonathan set his drink down on an end table and began to pace. "Please don't laugh at me if I ask stupid questions," he said to Ahmay.

Ahmay swallowed a smirk. "Ahmay promise," he said straight–faced. "No laughing at stupid questions."

Jonathan rolled his eyes and glared at the Shoshone chief.

"Sorry; it just slipped out," Ahmay said, hunching one shoulder and cocking his head to one side in feigned embarrassment. "No more stupid comments, either."

"Anyway, I have two questions. First, do I really have the power to heal my finger, right now?"

Ahmay thought for a minute. "Before I give you a direct answer, you need more information so that what I say will make sense." He gestured toward a couch. "Sit down and relax. When you pace I feel nervous."

Jonathan sat down.

"Let us go back to what you and Ramda talked about just before we took a break: thought. Ramda told you that thought creates form, and he gave examples of how thoughts create form within your being as well as in the outside world."

"Right," said Jonathan, "but I have a question about that, too. Does he really mean create in the sense that, where there was once nothing, there is now something, or, does he actually mean something quite different?"

Ahmay thought for a moment. "You really do ask good questions, young Bear. I am impressed. There can be no doubt that the English language has limitations; this whole question is a lot easier to answer in Shoshone. What Ramda was trying to communicate had to do with the effect of thought on energy.

"Obviously, none of us 'create' energy. That is one of the Universal Principles: Energy Just Is. What thought does do is give energy a new vibrational frequency, which then produces a rippling effect within the Universe. Those rippling effects could be said to be new creations because they are new and unique for that moment. However, if you really want to be precise, thought produces or designs form by re–utilizing that which already is: energy." Ahmay paused to study Jonathan. "Does that help you?"

The visitor nodded.

"So," continued Ahmay, "thought designs form, and that is just the tip of the iceberg in terms of the power humans have. They have the capability to control and direct not only their thoughts, feelings, and actions, but so much more."

"Like what?" Jonathan remarked.

"Like everything. In other words, you are in charge, whether you know it or not. It starts with a knowingness that you have designed it all and continues with a willingness to accept full responsibility for the results. Blaming your parents or your neighborhood or your school or fate or anyone else but yourself is a formula for continued imbalance."

Jonathan stood up and began pacing. "Let me get this straight. Are you saying that everything that's happened in my life is a result of things I have done, decisions I have made?"

Ahmay nodded. "Exactly. It is your design; it is your blueprint; it is your production. Use any metaphor you want, but you are the boss. You have done some acting, Jonathan, let us try a theatrical metaphor.

"Divine Reality is the producer, in that it provides an endless flow of energy, but everything else is up to you. You write the script, choose your role, select the players, choose the lighting, props, and scenery, as well as direct how all these elements are to be coordinated into one seamless, theatrical journey or adventure." Ahmay paused.

Jonathan kept pacing, staring at the new plush carpet, hands behind his back. "Go on, go on," he said.

"Carrying the theatrical metaphor even further," said Ahmay, "eternity for you, the metaphorical director, is like being in charge of an eternal repertory production company. As soon as one production ends, it is time to begin another. It never ends."

"Wait a minute, are you telling me that life for humans on Earth can be compared to one theater production after another, each lifetime being synonymous with one production?"

"That is exactly what I am saying," said Ahmay.

"Hmmmm." Jonathan sat down and stared at the ceiling. "I'm going to have to think about that one." He picked up his "beer" and took a long drink. "You're talking about reincarnation," he blurted.

Ahmay nodded.

"So what's the point?" Jonathan wondered, watching the particles of dust in the beam of light. "Why do we choose to have all these lives?"

"Choose is exactly the right word. You chose to learn. Remember the purpose of your existence is to move toward balance. Your life is about awareness and learning. Learning and knowledge promote balance; all life naturally aspires to perfect balance; perfect balance is the Divine Reality and that which motivates all life."

Jonathan got off the couch and sat on the floor in a lotus position. He focused on the light beam. Taylor, you've got to concentrate, he told himself. The answer to your problem with your finger and possibly the transition section of your concerto may be just a question or two away. "What happened to Heaven and Hell," he asked, "and God and the uniqueness of each life and each soul?"

Ahmay shook his head. "Young Bear, one thing I like about you is that when you ask a question, you do not fool around.

"Let us start at the top: there is no Heaven or Hell. The Celestial Bar is not Heaven; it is a recycling and information center for spirits. Heaven and Hell as places are inventions of those who believe in separateness. Since focus produces reality, that is their reality. Universal Principles transcend the notion of separateness: everyone and everything is connected by their essence, namely energy and the Oneness of our spirits. Therefore, there can be no actual separateness.

"So," Ahmay concluded, "that leaves unanswered your question about God and the uniqueness of each life and each soul."

Suddenly, a strange noise came from the light beam. It sounded like coughing. "Excuse me," blared Ramda's deep voice, "but I would like to get in on this part of your discussion, if I may."

"Please do," said Ahmay, "Jonathan keeps asking all these complicated questions. An old Shoshone like me is not used to having to explain these questions in English."

"The problem with any discussion of the word 'God,'" said Ramda, "is its definition or language. To define anything, at least in the English language, is to limit it. The next difficulty is your limited state of awareness. Most souls in physical form have difficulty in seeing themselves for who they truly are; nonetheless, trying to define God in all of Her/His glory. But for the purposes of our discussion, Jonathan, it would be easiest to say that here at the Celestial Bar, your Earth–concept of God would be pretty nearly synonymous with our Divine Reality. The biggest difference would be one of intent.

"On Earth, God or Allah or whatever other name one may choose, is generally considered to exercise an omniscient will—either actively or passively—in all that transpires. Here, Divine Reality has no will; it just is. It is the manifestation of perfection or perfect balance in all things, known and unknown. It is that to which all living things aspire. Ergo, Divine Reality."

Everyone was silent.

After a few moments Ramda added, "Just know that, whatever you believe God to be, He/She/It is infinitely more—more loving, more knowledgeable, more forgiving, more powerful, more compassionate, more ... more.

"Thanks for your help, Ramda," said Ahmay. "I hope that helps clarify things for our young visitor."

Jonathan sat, still studying the light beam. "But what about the uniqueness of each life and each soul?" he asked. "Without that, doesn't life itself become trivialized and meaningless?"

"Jonathan," boomed Ramda's voice, "subjective conclusions are not a part of what we do here at the Celestial Bar. Life is energy, uniquely designed by each soul for the purpose of learning. That is why you hear us use the phrase or term 'Earth School.' Judgments about that life are not a part of the Universal Principles under which we operate. All life either moves toward balance or away from balance; there are only two choices, but each life–design is unique and special, similar to each human's fingerprint or voiceprint. However, a particular life—or life–adventure or life–journey or whatever else you may choose to call it—is not an end unto itself. The end of that life—death as you call it on Earth—is not a calamitous event nor is it a joyful event. It is merely the end of one learning experience and the beginning of another."

Silence again filled the Transition Room as Jonathan continued to sit and stare at the light beam.

"Jonathan," Ramda said, "are we helping you?"

The visitor nodded, almost imperceptibly.

Ahmay watched him for several minutes before speaking. "And that brings us to the subject of the soul," he said, almost whispering. "I would like to address that subject for a few moments, young Bear."

Jonathan appeared almost inert.

Ahmay paused to compose his thoughts. "'Soul' is another word that requires definition before it can be effectively discussed. For us in the Celestial Bar, soul is that particle of light that, deep within, has an eternal awareness of the connection to the Oneness; it is the accumulated repository of all our learning experiences in our ongoing quest for perfect balance through one life–design after another, en route to a re-unification with the One: Divine Reality. That eternal quest we call, 'The Movement.'

"Let me use another analogy. 'The Movement' can be likened to a river that is flowing toward the ocean. As long as the basic laws of Earth's nature remain intact, nothing can prevent that river from eventually reaching the ocean. Even dams built to block its path will, with the fullness of time, collapse and the river will continue its journey. Shifts in land masses will, in the fullness of eternity, not prevail over that river; it will sooner or later reach the ocean. Such is the power and overwhelming single–mindedness of the soul, as we use that word.

"However," Ahmay continued, "we—Ramda and I and the rest of the staff—realize that you may have meant something else when you asked your question about the soul. If you were referring to the Earth people's notion of the soul—that popular misconception that soul is a separated part of God or Allah that comes with an Earth–life—we see that concept as part and parcel of separateness. As we discussed earlier, we view that idea as fatally flawed because it promotes disharmony and imbalance."

Ahmay paused. "Jonathan, do you understand?"

Jonathan scowled and remained inert for a few minutes before uncrossing his legs and standing up. He looked around the room, then down at his pinkie. "You mean to tell me, Ahmay," he said, bringing his hand up in front of his face to examine the crooked finger, "that my soul decided to do this as a learning experience?"

Ahmay grinned and shrugged his shoulders. "I realize it may sound funny to you, Jonathan, but that is precisely what I am telling you. And you know what? I think it is time we did something different, so you can grasp the whole concept we are trying to convey. The last person to audition before you in Los Angeles is halfway through her program. What do you think, Ramda; is it time to take him into virtual reality, Celestial Bar style?"

Jonathan was standing tensely before the light, his face grim as he thought about all the previous information.

"Groovy, dude. Totally radical," said Ramda.

Ahmay laughed—then caught himself. "Sorry, Jonathan," he said. "I am not laughing at you. But to see you look so serious, and then hear Ramda's off–the–wall remark—it is just plain funny."

"No problem."

"Do not take things so seriously, Jonathan. Okay?" Ahmay slapped him on the back.

"I'll try. So what is this virtual reality stuff? On Earth, it's kind of a toy they use in amusement parks or movies."

"Our virtual reality machine, will help you absorb a great deal of information in a very short period of time," Ahmay explained. "Any time you want out, all you have to say or even think is, 'I want this virtual reality to stop.'"

"Do I have enough time? We haven't resolved my music problem and this pinkie thing yet, and I want to talk to you about Paula. I need to see her again before I leave and there's something I have to ask you about her."

"I understand all that," Ahmay said soothingly. "I promise, all the subjects you have just mentioned will be covered in great detail before you leave, and you also will have ample time to be with Paula. Do not forget, young Bear, time in the Celestial Bar is completely different than on Earth. Everything that will happen to you during the rest of your visit here will take no more than a few moments in Earth time."

Jonathan chugged his beer, then took a deep breath. "I can't believe this place," he muttered to himself. "Okay, Ahmay," he said out loud, "I guess I'm ready. If I can't trust a Shoshone chieftain, then who can I trust?"

"Your friendly neighborhood computer," said Ramda.

"Ignore him." Ahmay smiled and walked over to the equipment center on the wall. "He is just giving you a hard time. Go ahead and step into his beam of light, and we will get things adjusted for you. It will just take a second."

Jonathan stepped into the light. At first he saw the colors flowing through his body, just like before. This time there were more colors, especially more pink coming from his chest.

"Don't worry or panic, if you feel yourself become someone else while you are in this virtual reality," Ahmay said as he adjusted knobs and flicked switches. "This machine has the ability to act as a time machine, in addition to its many other features. Just remember, this is a learning experience. Learnings occur in many different forms; some by reflecting, some by being told, some by being shown, and some by experiencing. We will allow nothing to hurt you. However, you may experience pain or sorrow or happiness or joy or surprise or ecstasy or even love. None of it is present reality. The instant you say or think, 'I want this virtual reality to stop,' all the sights, sounds, smells, tastes, and feelings you are experiencing will disappear, and you will be standing here with Ramda and me." Ahmay turned around to look at Jonathan. "You ready?"

Jonathan chuckled. "After that charming caveat, who could resist such a tempting prospect? I can hardly wait."

Ahmay laughed. "Well, at least you have not lost your sense of humor." He pushed a few more buttons. "Here goes."

Everything became dark. Jonathan felt as if he was awakening from sleep; he smelled smoke. He was in a bed.

There's a fire close–by, he thinks. Maybe it's in the bar, or possibly that equipment doesn't work nearly as well as Ahmay said. He feels panic. There's a real fire out there somewhere. He can hear it crackling and popping. The reflections of the flames flicker and dance on his bedroom walls. He tries calling out for Ramda and Ahmay, but hears the screams of a little girl come out of his mouth in Spanish. *"Miguel! Padre!"* she shouts out in a high, shrill voice.

She hurries from her bed and sees a reflection in the window; she's a little girl around ten or eleven. Outside, it's a clear spring dawn and hard to distinguish between the thin, red clouds and the burning flames that are billowing black smoke from the second floor of the family horse barn.

"Apollo," she whispers, thinking of her black-and-white pinto. The magnificent animal and she are inseparable companions from dawn to dusk. The girl considers the horse her only friend in the whole world. No one in her family has time for her. They're too busy working. Most days, she and Apollo ride for hours through the neighboring canyons, mountains, and streams—sharing their deepest secrets.

In a flash, the girl puts on her work pants and boots and rushes down the wooden stairs out into the chilly morning air. She heads for the barn door. She'll open it.

"Juanita," yells Miguel, her 15–year–old brother, running past her carrying two buckets of water, "stay away from the barn! It's too dangerous!"

Juanita sees her father running around the inside of the barn, throwing water and stomping out flames. The air is heavy with smoke, the sound of roaring flames, and the screams of horses frenzied with fear. She sees that the door leading from the barn to the corral area is closed.

She opens the outside gate to the corral and runs through it to unlock the barn door from the outside. As she opens the door, her usually gentle Apollo and several other horses leap through a cloud of inky smoke.

"Apollo!" she yells, seeing that he's heading for the open gate. She bolts after her friend, hoping to distract the pinto before he reaches the open gate. "Apollo!" she bellows as loud as she can. She doesn't see the other stampeding horses thundering toward her.

The first one tries to avoid her, but hits her with his chest and sends her flying high into the air. As she comes back down and hits the ground, another terrified horse tries to miss her but runs over her, one hoof glancing her frail face. While she's rolling to a stop, another tramples over her, smashing her hip. Then another: its front hooves land squarely on her lower back, crushing her spine; the rear hooves shatter a thigh bone. The impact flips her onto her back. All she can see before losing consciousness is the white underbelly of the last horse as it jumps clear of her crumpled body.

"Juanita!" screams her father, running from the burning barn; Miguel is close behind.

Now the sturdy pinto stops, watches as the other horses bolt to freedom, then trots back to be with his fallen friend, whinnying and licking her bloodied face.

Now it's dark.

Juanita feels herself waking up in a bed again. She opens her eyes. It's the end of a different day. Miguel is lighting candles around her bedroom; they're the only source of light. It's blistering hot. She's in her own bedroom and her own wooden bed. Her father and brother have worried looks on their faces. There's a strange stench in the air. Thick gauze wrappings run out from under her damp nightgown, down the full length of her badly swollen legs.

The only flesh she can see are puffy toes sticking out from bandages around her feet. The skin is dark green.

Her head aches so badly, tears stream down her cheeks; her whole body throbs. She moves one hand to wipe away the tears and feels a big bandage around her head and one cheek. She's covered with sweat and her breathing is labored. Each breath is accompanied by a heavy, gurgling in her chest and throat.

Miguel pours water from a clay pitcher into a small wooden cup and brings it to her. "Drink this," he says, lifting Juanita's head and putting the cup to her dry lips.

The girl tries to drink, but the pain in her head and body is so sharp, she can barely find the strength. She only manages a few swallows.

Juanita senses the concern and love in her brother's eyes. She feels the anguish he's built over the last few weeks—wanting to help, wanting to take the pain away.

Her father removes a small bottle from her dresser and pours something into another cup. It smells like alcohol. He brings it to her and lifts her head. "This will help with the pain," he whispers. "It's all we've got, little girl. I'm sorry."

She manages only one swallow; it tastes awful. Her father sets her head back down on the pillow and her brother hands him a wet towel. Gently, her father wipes her sweat–covered face and arms. That feels a little better for a moment or two. Miguel comes with another wet cloth and places it on her forehead. That feels even better.

She closes her eyes and realizes how weak she is. Just that small amount of moving has left her out of breath and wheezing even more than before. More tears run down her cheeks. She wishes she could fall asleep until she is well.

"When is the priest coming?" she hears her father ask.

"Right after vespers," her brother whispers.

The room gets quiet as her brother and father leave. Juanita feels as if she's ready to fall back asleep, when something makes her open her eyes. At the corner of her bed she sees the translucent figure of a stranger. It's a woman. At that moment, the girl starts shivering from head to toe. The tall, blonde woman comes closer and touches the girl's hand.

Jonathan recognizes the visitor: it's Paula.

The girl and Paula begin to float. Instantly, they're going down a long tunnel of light, and then there's a whooshing sound.

"I'm fast–forwarding," said Ahmay. "This portion is not for your experience, now."

Suddenly, Juanita was in a beautiful park, standing beside Paula. The little girl had long, black hair and dark skin. To Jonathan she appeared small for her age with a cute face, green eyes, and a pouty mouth. Dressed in play shorts and blouse, she looked down at her healed legs. "I'm all better."

Paula smiled and bent over to look Juanita in the eye. "As long as we are here, you will feel no pain and nothing will happen to you that you do not want. Understand?"

Juanita nodded and ran off to play with some other children her own age who were playing on a Jungle Gym.

Paula sat on a bench and watched.

A few minutes later, Juanita ran back to Paula and jumped into her lap. "You know what? I love you, Paula."

Paula's eyes misted. "I am sure you do," she said. "And I love you, too; more than you know."

They hugged each other for a long time before Juanita jumped up and ran back to play with her new friends. Jonathan smiled as he watched, for what seemed like hours, as the young girl ran and ran.

Then Jonathan heard the whooshing noise again.

Paula and Juanita were holding hands and walking toward The Celestial Bar. "Is this where you work?" asked the little girl.

"For now," answered Paula, smiling.

Once inside, Juanita was greeted like a long-lost niece by many of the patrons. They came up and gave her hugs and kisses. Zorinthalian ran up, picked her up, kissed her, and twirled her in the air. He took her and Paula to a booth beside the bar and brought hot food and a drink.

Before he left for his duties behind the bar, he gave Juanita another kiss on the cheek.

Shortly, he returned with a special Celestial Bar ice cream shake and two straws. The two women guzzled down the drink while laughing and joking. Then they got up and started down the hallway toward the transition rooms, hand in hand.

Again Jonathan heard the whooshing sound. He saw both of them walking back from the transition room area. There was something different about Juanita. She didn't seem like the little girl who had been running in the park; there was a sense of knowingness about her.

Then there was another whooshing noise. "It is many Earth years later," said Ahmay in the background.

Juanita was back in the bar and looked disappointed. "I'm sorry," said one of her women friends. "It would have been great to be with you again, but I don't think our learning lessons are that compatible this time."

"I know," said Juanita as she hugged the woman. "But I'm still disappointed. Maybe next time."

Juanita went off to talk with some more of her friends at the bar. She started speaking with two men.

As Jonathan watched the interaction, he felt a flood of emotions move through him. One man, by the name of Tamrin, was quite tall with big shoulders, a deep voice, and an aura that commanded respect. The second man, named Sashiko, was mild–mannered and soft-spoken. Jonathan wanted to tell this man something—something very important—but he didn't know what it would be. He sat there and watched the scenario unfold.

The two men explained to Juanita that they were about to incarnate. They had several issues to learn from each other, many of which were unresolved from previous lifetimes. The main issue they were going to work on was that of power: Tamrin was going to attempt to let go of his need to control through power; Sashiko was to learn to establish power and let go of his fear of it. Together, they would learn from each other.

Tamrin and Sashiko had already decided on their parents, who had already returned to Earth School. Both would end up with families in Chicago. They would meet there, get married, and have one child, a boy. They asked if Juanita would like to join them and be their child.

Juanita thought for a moment. She realized that loneliness was an unresolved issue left over from her last trip to Earth School. Back then, her parents had seldom had time for her; they were too busy trying to work their horse farm and earn a living to worry about the needs of an 11–year–old. Abandonment was an issue Juanita felt like she needed to work on. That, and less focus on things physical, were the two main lessons she wanted to concentrate on during her next trip to Earth School.

"You mean spirituality?" asked Tamrin.

"Yes," said Juanita. "I think I need to learn to see things more in perspective and come to understand that the glue that holds everything together is our spirituality. Without it, our focus becomes distorted by our other vibrational frequencies."

"I agree," said Sashiko. "In fact that's something I want to work on as well."

"That makes it unanimous," said Tamrin.

The three joined hands.

"Then, we're agreed," said Tamrin. "I'll be the mother, Sashiko will be the father, and you'll be our son. What would you like your name to be?"

Juanita thought for a moment. "I think I'd like Jonathan," she said. "Jonathan has a nice ring to it."

Suddenly it was pitch dark.

"That is all for now," said Ahmay.

Jonathan stood in Ramda's beam of light, peering out at the tall Native American. He walked away from Ramda, out of the light, and sat down on a couch, shaking his head. The room was silent while he stared up at the ceiling. "Wow," he finally said. "That's all I can think of to say—wow. Unbelievable."

Chapter 11

" ... tragedy is an opportunity for another lesson; a gift ... "

Time seemed to stand still in Transition Room 6. No one spoke. Ramda's silent glare heated the air and ricocheted off the white paint. The only sound in the room was the gentle hum of the equipment on the wall.

Ahmay got up from his club chair, walked over to the refrigerator and got himself a "beer." He got one for Jonathan, too. The visitor from San Diego was deep in thought, lying on a couch, eyes closed.

"This will help," Ahmay told Jonathan, setting the can beside him. "Whenever you are ready." Ahmay sat down again, drank from his can, and closed his eyes.

"You know," said Jonathan, eyes still closed, voice groggy, "I realize that you've just exposed me to an entirely new way of looking at time and space and my own immortality, but I'm still not quite sure if I've figured out why it is that I designed the injury to my pinkie."

Ahmay choked on his drink. "You mean to tell me that," he said, half laughing—half choking, "that you have just experienced the multi–dimensionality of your soul, the dynamics of choice, the law about all 'Energy Moves in a Circular Fashion'—what you call reincarnation—and all you can think to talk about is your finger?"

Jonathan smiled sheepishly. "It's the only way I can cope. I can relate to my finger. Besides, my broken pinkie doesn't make any sense. Based on the deal I made with my parents, it should have something to do with spirituality or dependence on things physical. It certainly doesn't have anything to do with abandonment; that's for sure."

"Is that a question or a statement?" asked Ahmay.

"Either way," Jonathan said. "Am I right or wrong?"

Ahmay shook his head. "There you go again with that separateness stuff. Remember, we do not do separateness at the Celestial Bar. We do love, we do balance, and we do energy; we do learning, we do parent shopping, guide shopping, and soul grouping, but we do not do separateness. Separateness is about imbalance, and therefore, is a behavior guides do not choose.

"With respect to your direct question," Ahmay continued, "I want to tell you that I am your guide—what you might call a guardian angel—not your personal answer man or universal encyclopedia. Guides do guiding, not fortune-telling, not therapy, and definitely not judgment–making. One of the hardest things for a guide is to let go. We have to learn to allow our students to make choices that oftentimes produce disharmony or imbalance; that is a vital part of their learning process."

Ahmay took a sip of his beer. "So now, Jonathan, why not tell me why you decided to break your finger and then not let it heal properly? I would like to hear your answer."

Jonathan made a face by turning down the corners of his mouth, then shrugging. "The truth is I have no idea," he said, "that's why I asked you. I thought if I knew why I did it, I could more easily figure out what I could do to remove whatever blockage was preventing its complete recovery."

Ahmay smiled. "You should remember a couple of things: that wherever you are in the present is because of your past, and that the body manifests the balance or imbalance of the emotional, intellectual, and spiritual aspects of yourself. All I can tell you is that you are on the right track. Keep working at it; you are almost there."

Jonathan grinned, too. "All right, Mr. Shoshone chieftain with the long black hair, how about an answer you can give me? How'd you get to be my guide?"

"That is easy," said Ahmay, "like everything else, you chose me. In effect, we chose each other. Right after you and your future parents decided on your next life-design, you placed an ad here for a Spiritual Guide. About two dozen of us responded and you chose me."

"I see," Jonathan said. "I'd like to know more about you and Ramda. Who were you before you became guides?"

Ramda cleared his throat. An image of a man dressed in robes appeared in Ramda's beam of light. He was tall and statuesque and handsome; his skin was tough, wrinkled, and tanned from the sun. "This was my last costume when I was on Earth. I spent most of my time in the Middle East—Egypt actually. That was over two thousand Earth years ago, and at that time I was called a seer." The image disappeared. "But that was just one of many lifetimes that I have enjoyed. Now I am a master teacher—my job is to help raise the vibrational frequency of the mass consciousness."

"My role is to be your personal guide. I am here to help you change your own consciousness," Ahmay said. "As you know, I was a Shoshone chieftain roaming the Northwest plains most recently. And, same as Ramda, I have had many lifetimes before that."

"So why do you present yourself to me as a Native American and why does Ramda present himself as a beam of light?"

"Two main reasons," said Ahmay. "One, we are all part of the same soul group. Two, to make our guidance as relevant as possible to your needs at this particular moment. The former makes the latter all the easier to decide. In other words, we are convinced the form we have chosen will be the most beneficial to you, in terms of your needs for the moment."

"What is a soul group?" asked Jonathan.

"They are an association or co–op of souls," said Ramda, "who decide for reasons of convenience or sympathetic vibrations or similar backgrounds or whatever to become like that repertory theater group we discussed. They all keep changing roles, with the expectation that they can help each other learn more because they know each other so well. Everyone takes all their stuff with them into the physical or spiritual worlds, no matter how many lives they have or where they are living out their next life. Not only that, each knows why the other has designed a particular life format or play. Members of the same soul group agree to be in each other's plays. We are all here to help each other."

"So what are you guys getting out of this?"

"Do not forget, you are helping me, too," said Ahmay. "By teaching a particular lesson, I become more in balance and I also learn to become a better teacher."

Ahmay finished his drink and carried it to the trash can. "Ramda, Paula, Mark, and I, are all part of your soul group. So are your parents, many of your friends, and most of your intimate relationships. Did you realize that Juanita's father is Judy and that Miguel, her brother, is Mary? One of the reasons you were drawn into staying in Key West and setting up a restaurant with Judy was to finish some old business the two of you had acquired over your past lifetimes."

"Then why did I feel so much pain in the last two years before the restaurant sank?"

"You had learned your lesson and were ready to move on, but didn't," Ahmay replied.

"Well, Judy wouldn't sell the boat, so it seems that she hadn't learned hers yet," Jonathan added, a little defensively.

"Yes, that was true. But was that any reason for you to continue in the relationship? Do not worry Jonathan, that is a very common occurrence in learning lessons. One person learns their lesson before the other but does not recognize that fact, so they continue in the same situation. When the pain gets too much, they eventually leave. By the way, she is well advanced in other lessons where you are still a beginner."

Jonathan changed the subject. "What about ... "

"Mary." Ahmay interjected. "I would rather not say. There are a few more surprises waiting for you on Earth; I do not want to ruin them."

Jonathan thought of a part of the virtual reality where Juanita—well, really himself—was parent shopping. "I can't believe my mother is part of my soul group. That was a real surprise."

"You witnessed the moment you decided to be in each others' production."

"I know." Jonathan, shook his head. "I've got a lot of catching up to do there, as well. Whew. When I get back, I've got to figure out why I chose my mother."

Taylor, he thought to himself, do you realize if the people on Earth knew they chose their families, it would turn the field of psychotherapy upside–down? The mind boggles.

"Now you are getting it, Young Bear," Ahmay chuckled. "That is my new name for you."

Jonathan nodded respectfully. "Thank you. And what's your plan for me?" Jonathan asked. "Educate me, show me, shock me, inspire me, wake me up, keep me from falling into the porcelain fixture, or just get me to think?"

Ahmay shrugged and thought for a moment. "All of the above."

"Since I designed my life, this visit to the Celestial Bar must be part of that design," Jonathan realized.

Ahmay nodded.

"And I must be here to learn something," he added. "The $64,000 question is, what?" He paused, deep in thought. "When you answered 'all of the above,' what exactly did that mean? In the final analysis, all you're really trying to do is help get me more in balance. Isn't that it? Is that how you help me, through my vibrational frequencies?"

Ahmay grinned. "Now you are cooking, Young Bear. My main job is exactly that: to help you raise your individual VF. That is how I can give you the most service."

For a split second, Jonathan recalled his conversation with Zorinthalian about servers, then re–focused to the moment. "But first, comes remembering. Then I've got to want it. Right?"

"That is half of it. The other half involves behavior: you have to raise your own VF by putting yourself into a higher state of balance, by letting go of blockages. By coming here in the middle of this life–design, you proved you were serious. The last part is the acting on it. Already, Young Bear, you have made much progress."

"What else can I do?" asked Jonathan.

"Let us go back to your visit to virtual reality," said Ahmay. "What do you think about all that?"

Jonathan shook his head and felt his eyes misting. He swallowed and tried to clear his throat. "Very powerful." His voice cracked. "It just ... blew ... me away."

"What was so very powerful about it?" asked Ahmay.

"Well ... first off, there was Paula. I know now that she was one of my guides in my last lifetime, but that doesn't change how I feel toward her. I also realize that's one of my main blockages; she as much as told me so beside the piano. So that's a very powerful and painful message. I know I have to resolve that before I go back and that's why I want a chance to speak with her alone."

Ahmay nodded. "And I have assured you it will happen."

"Yes, you have, and I appreciate it." Jonathan got up and began to pace. "There were also a couple of little mysteries about my life that I believe were solved. After seeing what happened to me, as Juanita, I understand my love for running and also my fear of on-coming traffic."

"Another aspect of the residual effects of past lives, especially the most recent ones," Ahmay agreed.

"But there was an aspect of that virtual reality that really bothered me."

"What was that?"

"That little girl died—okay me—and left a grieving family behind, and all that virtual reality clip concerned itself with was Juanita and her pain and suffering and how things changed for her at the Celestial Bar. What about her brother and father—ahhh, I mean, Mary and Judy? They were the closest to her at the moment of the accident. Imagine their pain! Imagine their devastation! Both of them probably spent the rest of their lives blaming themselves."

"Like you, with your dad?" asked Ahmay.

Jonathan fell silent. He'd been blind-sided. "Kind of," stumbled Jonathan. He didn't want to deal with that issue, at least not now. "Not only that, but it wasn't their fault, yet they had to suffer the most pain. Juanita was fine; she was dead. Her physical and mental pain were over, but her family's was just beginning. What do your Universal Principles have to say about that?"

"Ramda," Ahmay called out. "Ramda, I need your help."

"Coming, Mother," boomed the computer's deep voice.

Ahmay rolled his eyes at Ramda's attempted humor. "Our friend from San Diego needs some of your expert insights vis-a-vis tragedy and why it sometimes happens to bystanders."

"Certainly," said Ramda. "Jonathan, you remember earlier when you and I were talking about how subjective conclusions are not part of what we do here at the Celestial Bar?"

Jonathan nodded.

"We were talking about death at that time," Ramda continued, "and how a particular life or life–design was not an end in itself, that death was neither a calamitous nor joyful event; it was merely the end of one life and the continuation of your soul life—a learning opportunity, if you will. Actually, that example fairly characterizes the role tragedy plays in all life–design: tragedy is an opportunity for another lesson; a gift, even."

"A gift?" Jonathan blurted. "You've got to be kidding! Tell that to Juanita's brother or father. Tell that to

California urban parents who watch in horror as their children are murdered before their very eyes by drive–by killers; tell that to parents who watch their children starve to death in Africa or India or Central America; tell that to the families of Bosnia who watched helplessly as their loved ones were taken out into the streets by cold–blooded soldiers and butchered. If that's a gift, you can keep it!"

Ramda cleared his throat. "Jonathan," he said, his voice gentle yet compelling, "please listen carefully to my words. My words are words of love. You will talk of love in more detail with Paula; she is one of the best guides in the universe on the subject of love. But everything we do here at the Celestial Bar is about love. Everything. My ideas are about love and caring and nurturing and balance and harmony; same with Ahmay and his area of expertise, spirituality; same with Mark and his powerful knowledge of your body. The glue or the common thread for all that we do here is love. You must know that, at least at an intellectual level."

"I do believe that," said Jonathan. "To the depths of my being, I believe that."

"All right, then," sighed Ramda, "now we have a starting point. So, love is about harmony and balance. Balance is about learning; that is why individuals design their lives: to learn balance. A part of that learning process includes learning from tragedy because it is an integral part of the life experience.

"That is not to denigrate or trivialize the pain and suffering tragedy inflicts. It is a deeply traumatic and scarring occurrence. I speak from first–hand personal knowledge, but that is another issue. The point is that it hurts and distracts. The temptation is to let your perspective of tragedy only focus on the physical reality, when the truth is tragedy is not Reality; it is a reflection of Reality. The truth is, tragedy is a perfect example of thought producing form. A corollary to this whole discussion of tragedy is 'Energy is Limitless and Powerful'—another Law of Energy. If tragedy is allowed to become more powerful than life itself, then that is what it will be. If, with your thoughts, you design tragedy to be an overpowering monster, then that is what it will become.

"However," Ramda said, clearing his throat, "if tragedy is viewed as another opportunity in life for growth and learning, then it becomes more manageable and empowering and more capable of producing balance. If your thoughts or 'attitude' are that through the use of the limitlessness and power of energy, you can use it as another learning experience, then you will take a giant step toward harmony and balance."

Jonathan stopped his pacing, sat down, and gulped down his drink. He crumpled the empty can with one hand and tossed it into a trash can beside his chair. "That's easy to talk about and intellectualize, Ramda," he said, "but not much help when you're in the middle of trying to cope."

"Attitude is everything," Ramda said. "Did you ever see the movie, 'Lawrence of Arabia'?"

Jonathan grunted.

"There is a scene with Lawrence—early in the movie—when he is still stationed in Cairo as an officer and a gentleman, and he learns he is to be sent into the Arabian desert on a diplomatic mission because he speaks the language. He has never been there nor exposed to the rigors of the desert before. A buddy asks him how he plans to handle the lack of water and the heat. Lawrence responds by lighting a wooden match, letting it burn down to where it begins to burn his fingers, and then putting it out with the bare fingers of his other hand.

"His buddy asks, 'How can you do that? Doesn't it hurt?'

"Lawrence replies, 'Of course it hurts. The secret is not minding that it hurts.'"

Jonathan shook his head. "I'm going to have to think about this tragedy business some more, I've got too much time and habit invested in the blame game. It's extremely hard to just come here and have you and Ahmay tell me that I've got an attitude problem when it comes to pain and suffering, and then simply stop what I've been doing for 37 years. It takes some heavy–duty concentration on the Universal Principles."

"I respect that," said Ramda. "One last thought: tragedy can sometimes act to shake up our illusionary belief that form is reality. Form comes in all guises: color, race, religion, political beliefs, nationality, a house, wealth, youthful appearance, education, cultural heritage, or one's neighborhood. Again, tragedy will never make sense from purely a physical perspective.

"Tragedy has a way of assisting in the process of sifting through the perceived realities to arrive at the Divine Reality. It provides the gift of connecting spirit to spirit, when people let go of such heavy emphasis on the thought process and just act in harmony, like the way people helped each other in the recent Los Angeles earthquake and, before that, the floods of the Midwest and the hurricanes on the East coast. When people just let go and act, their spirit has an opportunity to move toward connection and balance."

Ramda paused. "Remember, Jonathan, to include these concepts in your thoughts when you give further and more insightful consideration to this subject."

"I have something to add here, too," said Ahmay. "Rarely is an important lesson learned in one lifetime. Also, many times the learning comes after the experience, after there is time to put it in perspective and understand the learning. Once one has understood the learning, one then can create an experience like another earth lifetime, and then act on it. That gives one the opportunity to use that knowledge. As one acts on that knowledge in a PEISful—physical, emotional, intellectual, and spiritual— way, then one really knows that lesson. That is when life moves more smoothly, more freely toward harmony and balance."

Jonathan stood up. "I think I've just about hit system overload and, I'm almost out of time. I need to go see

Paula." As he turned toward the door he added, "Thanks, Ramda."

Jonathan hurried with Ahmay up the corridor toward the bar and restaurant. "When does Paula's shift end?"

"Any minute," Ahmay said, keeping stride with the younger man. "Want me to go find her for you?"

"Yes, please, thanks. I'll be at the bar. I want to ask Zorinthalian something."

"You be sure and say goodbye before you leave," Ahmay said.

"Don't worry," Jonathan assured him.

When he arrived at the bar, Zorinthalian was busy waiting on some other customers. Two of them stared at Jonathan and, as he sat down, they waved. They looked kind of familiar to him, so he half–heartedly waved back.

"Do you not recognize them?" said Zorinthalian, placing a bowl of munchies in front of Jonathan.

The visitor shook his head no.

The bartender smiled. "That is amazing," he said. "As many times as you have been in here, I would never have guessed you would not remember those two." He paused and took a deep breath. "All things in good time ... What did you want to ask me?"

Jonathan swallowed a smile. He was still not completely comfortable having most everyone here read his thoughts. "Are you one of my guides?"

Zorinthalian raised his eyebrows. "I am impressed by your directness," he said, looking the visitor straight in the eye. "No, I am not one of your guides, not yet. But let me show you something."

He walked out from behind the bar and went to one of the shields on the wall. It was the one Jonathan had particularly noticed when he first arrived. The shield had triangles on it with lines running through them that reminded him of smoothed–out lightning bolts.

Zorinthalian waved Jonathan over. "This shield is from a very special place in the universe," he said, carefully studying Jonathan's face. "What do you think of it?"

The visitor was oblivious to the bartender's scrutiny. He stared at the shield, closely inspecting its inter–looped circular emblem in the right–hand corner. Easy, Taylor, he reminded himself. Don't get excited over that creeping anxiety you're feeling right now. This guy's okay. Something weird is happening, but you've got to relax.

"There's something hauntingly familiar about it," Jonathan said. "My eyes were drawn to this shield the moment I saw it."

Zorinthalian pointed at it. "This is from my home," he said.

For the first time, Jonathan noticed that Zorinthalian's hand was different than his: a thumb and five fingers. A tingling sensation flowed through Jonathan and he could read Zorinthalian's thoughts—some of them. The bartender was trying to decide how much to tell Jonathan.

"Who are you really?" Jonathan blurted out.

"We will get to that," Zorinthalian said. "Tell me, did Ahmay use the analogy of Earth being like a school?"

Jonathan nodded.

"Well, you should know that there are lots of other schools throughout the universe," he said. "Actually millions of other schools, depending upon what lessons you are trying to learn. Most recently, you have chosen Earth School."

Keep it together now, Taylor. Take a few seconds to think this thing through before you come unglued. He forced himself to swallow. "What was my school before Earth?"

Zorinthalian smiled. "When the time comes, you will know the answer to that question. All I can tell you now is that my home is in the Seven Sisters—the Pleiades." He stopped and gave Jonathan a long stare.

Jonathan studied the tall, hulking man. "Well, how would you characterize who you are?"

"Everyone comes from someplace else," said Zorinthalian in a normal voice, "just like the genealogy of the United States is composed of all nationalities, religions, and ethnicity, so, too, is the Milky Way—only the frame of reference is the universe.

"We are all trying to go back home to the Oneness," continued Zorinthalian, "That is why Earth is such a popular school for learning, especially the United States. America's motto is *E Pluribus Unum*, which means, as you know, 'Out of Many, There is One.' That is also what is happening in all the universe: everyone is trying to find their way to balance which, when perfected, means we will all join in the Oneness.

"So, in answer to your question, who am I—I am a traveler from another place and time."

Jonathan stood there beside the tall, muscular man he called Zorinthalian and stared, dumbfounded, at the shield. You can't call him a liar, Taylor, he thought; there's too much proof that he's not a liar. Yet to accept what he's saying at face value is hard to grasp. How can all this be?

"When you are ready," Zorinthalian said, "I will work with you to show you the way back to full utilization of your talents. Now that you know the Universal Principles, it should be easier. First, you must get into your own balance."

"How do I do that?" Jonathan asked out loud.

"Live the Universal Principles," said the man with the unusual hands. "That will take more courage, patience, and persistence than you have ever had to use before. Before I can work through you, you will need to be able to handle an even higher vibrational frequency than Ramda's."

"What kinds of things will you be working on with me?"

"You are still unaware of many things: your distant past history, many of your future learning lessons, and your latent abilities and talents. So it would not make sense to you now," said Zorinthalian. "Suffice it to say that I will send you information on your heritage, on healing, and on how to further your purpose. Know for now that you and others have prepared long and hard for this period of Earth's development. The same drama that has been unfolding there has been unfolding at the cosmic level; the stage has been set for the multi–dimensional players and events. Now is the time for your hard labor to come to fruition."

Jonathan studied the insignia on the shield. Suddenly, something clicked into place within his thoughts. The four interconnected circles on the shield seem to represent the same concept Ahmay and Jonathan's other guides had been drumming into his head: PEIS. That's where it's at, he told himself, and that's where he'd been short–changing the emotional and the spiritual aspects of who he is.

Zorinthalian beamed. "You have it exactly right, Young Bear," he said. "Do you mind if I borrow Ahmay's nickname for you?"

Jonathan shook his head no.

"Good," said the bartender. He turned, gave Jonathan a quick hug, and then released him. Raw strength and energy from the man's hands and arms raced through Jonathan like a runaway locomotive; goosebumps covered his body. He was in the presence of quiet magnificence, he thought, a gentle, yet powerful server.

"I am most proud of you, my friend," said Zorinthalian, standing back and studying the visitor. "Your analysis of why it is you came here shows great insight. Your lessons during this visit are not over yet, but your willingness to listen and re–process old and new information is quite remarkable. I wish all our visitors were so open–minded."

He paused and thought, then pointed back to the shield. "This symbol will come to you on Earth at the right time and the right place. When it does, it will act as a key to unlock what has occurred here. Until then," Zorinthalian nodded stiffly, stepped to one side, and returned to the bar.

Jonathan stared at the bartender in utter awe. I wonder who he really is? Hope I get to find out some day. My time here must be almost up. Wonder what happened to Ahmay? Said he was going to find Paula for me. Sure would be nice to have some time with her. I've so much to tell her.

"Why not tell me now?" asked a melodious, female voice from directly behind him.

He whirled to see who it was.

It was Paula.

Chapter 12

"Love ... is not out there somewhere ... (it) is a choice and it is everywhere."

Paula's long blonde hair was combed down from the bun and it shined in the unusual light of the bar. She had changed out of her uniform and blouse into a lovely sun dress. "Well," she said, reaching for Jonathan's hand, "shall we go for a walk?"

Jonathan felt his heart jump, and he swallowed because his throat was suddenly too dry to speak. "I'd like that," he managed to get out.

She led him outside into the still night.

He gazed up into the darkness that was well-lit by the bright stars; they were the brightest he'd ever seen. There was no moon, but he noticed both their shadows on the soft grass as they strolled through the lush park.

Paula stopped and kissed him softly on the cheek. "It's so good to see you again, Jonathan."

He stared at her, speechless and confused. His heart raced, and he ached from wanting to take her in his arms and hold her and kiss her as he had in times past. He couldn't decide if he should jump with joy or prepare for sadness and disappointment; there was something ominous about the way she was acting: she was trying too hard to put him at ease.

"I'm not really clear about who we are to each other," he said, taking a deep breath and returning her look. "I know we're part of the same soul group, and I know you were kind of my guardian angel when I was Juanita. Beyond that, I really don't understand what's going on."

"Even after your chat with Ramda and Ahmay?" Paula was steering him down a pathway through the park. The evening was warm and balmy. A gentle breeze rustled the trees and tossed hair into Paula's beautiful face.

"That's right," he said, feeling a little foolish that he didn't understand, "even after my talk with them."

She looked up into the sky and pointed.

With his eyes, he took a picture of her stunning profile silhouetted in the starlight: strong nose, full lips and a happy mouth, large whimsical eyes, and a firm, yet gentle jawline. He felt love welling up deep within his soul— something he hadn't felt in a long, long time.

"You are not paying attention," she said sweetly.

"Sorry," he apologized, looking up into the sky.

"I just love looking at the stars." She turned to study him for a moment. "In fact, it is one of my most favorite things to do."

Jonathan returned her stare, then looked back up at the stars. His mind flashed to his many long evenings watching the stars from the breakwater. "Me, too," he said quietly.

"Of course," she said. "We are twin–flames, Jonathan. Did you not know?" He shook his head no. A gurgling stream was just ahead and he motioned that he wanted for them to rest there. They found a tall boulder with one flat side facing the water and sat side–by–side on the ground with their backs against the stone.

"What are twin–flames?" he asked.

"Twin–flames," she said, taking his hand again, "are two spirit–soul energies with almost identical vibrational frequencies. Many other energies—or in your case, people—have vibrational frequencies that are very close to yours, but twin–flames are the closest. We," she paused to kiss him on the cheek again, "are twin–flames. Have been for many a millennia."

Jonathan held his face with both hands, shaking his head. "This is so unbelievable," he said, "I can barely find the words to express myself. First, I'm energy that keeps reincarnating, then I'm part of a soul group that keeps learning together for all eternity, and, then, oh, by the way, I now have a twin–flame: someone who travels through time and space with me for all eternity, and who is closer to me than anyone else in all of creation." He took her hand and stared up into the clear sky, shaking his head. "I'm whining, aren't I?" He paused again. "Does that mean we have the same energy?"

She smiled. "Yes and no," she said, brushing hair from her eyes. "All energy is from the same source—the Oneness. You and I do have an ongoing conscious awareness of each other. So, in that sense, we are also connected or have the same energy. But, in another way, our energies are complementary: if you put both our energies together, we make a whole—you on the right, me on the left or visa versa; you as the woman, me as the man or visa versa. It is not so much a gender thing as it is complementary attributes as exemplified by the male and female of the human species."

He turned to look at her. In a whisper he blurted, "You're all I've been able to think about since I first saw you in the bar. I feel so close to you, closer than anyone. I just want to hold you and kiss you and love you."

"I know you do," she said, turning to face him. Their noses were only inches apart.

"I feel that we have been lovers. I've really seen and felt all those memories."

"You are absolutely right," she said, "and we were great. But what is important is not so much the physical aspects of our past or future love–making, but the love being expressed. Remember, being on Earth is about learning; it is not a vacation. It is about challenges and choices. You want to grow, you have to pay the price in terms of personal discipline and sacrifice. That doesn't mean you have to live a life of misery; it does mean you must learn to feel love in all things, including those things that are hard for you."

"The best gift of love, you could give me and yourself," Paula continued, her lips almost touching his, "would be to emotionally and intellectually let go of me when you go back. You are making it doubly hard on both of us and you are blocking yourself. You have been unconsciously comparing the women you date to me. That makes it almost impossible for you to have a healthy relationship with any woman. No one can compete with a ghost, nor should they have to. It is not fair to the women; it is not fair to me. But most of all, it is not fair to you."

Jonathan felt his heart racing, goosebumps covered his body, and his lips tingled. He couldn't resist. He reached over, closed his eyes, and kissed her on the lips. She returned the kiss, and they embraced and kissed some more. Each kiss was longer and more intimate. Every cell in his body danced with joy and delight. He opened his eyes and saw a pink glow engulfing both of them.

Startled, he jumped up and pulled away. The pink energy stayed with Paula, but now shrunk to about the size of a soccer ball on her chest. She took it into her hands and moved them around the outside of the light field in a small circular motion; it looked as if she were petting a small, furry animal.

"What is that?" he asked.

"This is love," she replied, holding it with care. "Actually, it is a manifestation of love in the form of a light field. More precisely, it is a manifestation of our love." She held out her hand to him. "Come on and touch it; it will not hurt you."

He knelt down and gave her his hand. She brought their hands to the outside of the light. Tenderly, he touched it and felt something, but he was not quite sure what. It kind of reminded him of an air curtain. He put his hand inside the pink light and felt a warm and relaxing, tingling sensation which quickly swept through his being and overwhelmed him with feelings of greater love for this woman—this "twin–flame." The pink ball of energy began to grow in size and intensity.

"It's alive," he said, sitting back down.

She smiled. "You are right. What you see here is always present in every moment in every part of this universe, in all universes. Love is the essence of everything. It is the fuel that propels the Movement within the both of us and all other living, conscious creatures. It is the life blood of all that is. It is just like what Ramda said to you earlier: 'Love is about harmony and balance.'"

He looked back up into the heavens. "If love is so wonderful," he said, "why is it so hard to find on Earth?"

"Lots of reasons," she said. "First, there is the word itself. When anyone tries to define the word 'love' in any other terms but the Universal Principles, they have problems. For instance, the sex act is often mistaken for love. Sex is not love; it is an activity that contains the potential for an expression of love. There is no better physical way for two people to express an intimate and deep love for each other. Because of that, sex and love are often mistaken to be one and the same. That is one of the main problems on Earth."

"Quite true," he said, "but that's not the only problem with finding love on Earth. It's much more complex than that."

Paula beamed. "I am so glad we are having this chat," she said, turning to face him. He gazed into her eyes. "You are perfectly correct. Love can be very complicated on Earth. To start with, there are different kinds of love: friendship, familial, a general love for all humankind and nature. Within those categories, there are enough gradations and subtleties to last several eternities, but there is one common denominator: these kinds of love can be best expressed in other aspects of oneself."

Jonathan added, "You mean PEIS; the physical, emotional, intellectual, and spiritual."

"That is exactly what I mean." Paula gently touched the side of his face. "The physical can be expressed in many ways: a caress, a look, a smile, a kiss.

"When people undergo an emotional connection with another person or part of nature, they experience care, concern, happiness, rapture, excitement, and warmth, to name a few." She looked down at her lap. "Like this pink ball of energy, the emotional manifestation of this love grows and grows as long as it is nurtured and fed by compassion, caring, and giving. So that is the emotional reason love on Earth is so complex.

"Then," Paula said, taking a deep breath and rubbing the ball of pink light, "then, there is the intellectual part, which requires pure acceptance or unconditional love—an act of will, some may call it. That is certainly no easy concept to put into action.

"And finally, there is the spiritual aspect of trying to discover love on Earth. That involves the conviction by humans that they are connected with the Oneness or the Divine Reality which in the final analysis is Perfect Love. With that conviction comes an inner peace and joy which permits all other aspects of the notion of love to naturally flow. Without it, feeling love on Earth is an almost impossible assignment.

"One more thing," she said. "The words 'finding love' are really a misnomer. Love on Earth is not out there somewhere, hiding or lost. Love is a choice and it is everywhere. Love is to be noticed and nurtured and cared for and shared. It is the sharing that makes it burn all the brighter."

She looked down at the ball of light. It had grown.

Jonathan was silent. The two of them closed their eyes and listened to the bubbling brook for a few minutes. He wanted to remember and cherish these moments for all time. Every second with Paula was filled with such magic.

"Part of the problem," he said, "is that on Earth, so much of what goes on is based on fear."

The pink ball began to shrink.

Paula nodded. "That is correct, but you cannot let that happen to you. All your energy needs to be focused on choosing love and removing any blockages. When that happens, your pathway through the darkness of indecision, uncertainty, and ignorance will be lit by the light of love and balance.

"Let us look at some manifestations of fear through PEIS: fear is felt in the physical as discomfort and pain; in emotions as loneliness and hate; in the intellect as bias and prejudice; in the spirit as emptiness and despair. But think of any fear: fear of flying, being in water, open spaces, closed spaces, black cats, public speaking, insects, dying, whatever. They all spring from a feeling of being disconnected. The antidote is knowledge and experience. In other words, Light. The Light of love for and with other humans."

Jonathan noticed the ball of light beginning to grow again. He chuckled. "I guess that's its way of wagging its tail. Sure is a sensitive little thing to words, though."

Paula smiled. "Words are important because they are the currency of thought. That is another problem with the situation on Earth: because of all the 21st-century technology, people have gotten sloppy about their communication skills. Poor communication leads to misunderstanding and imbalance, which leads to another point.

"There is a word in English called 'reflection.' It is another law of energy and a good term to describe a measuring device you can use to find out how things are going on Earth and, more specifically, with yourself."

"I hope I can remember all this stuff," he said.

"No problem," said Paula. "If you want to see how you are doing, compare your past to your present. Since you created it all, it is a perfect mirror for learning. When you are stumped by what you should be learning, look at how you are perceiving whoever is sitting across from you. If you wonder if you are a loving person, look into your heart and ask if you are sharing love with those around you. When you sense fear in others, look within to see where fear is hiding. If someone else's anger bothers you, check on what it is that is causing your anger."

"So the bottom line in using the 'Reflection Concept,' is that, to change the world, you must first change yourself?"

"Bin–go," Paula said in her best announcer voice. "Also, the best way to get anything you want—especially love—is to let go and live life to the fullest. Stop trying so hard to hold onto love." She got up and went to the stream. The light from the stars reflected brightly in the shallow, fast–moving water. She held the pink ball with one hand and motioned for Jonathan to join her beside the stream. "Let me show you something."

He moved over beside her and she handed him the pink ball of light. As their hands touched, the ball expanded and then shrank again when he held the ball by himself.

"See that big bubble floating downstream toward us?" she asked, pointing up the brook about twenty feet.

He nodded.

"Watch what happens," she said

When the bubble arrived, she cupped both hands and scooped it out of the flowing water, holding it in the palm of one hand. "Let us suppose this bubble represents a special love I have with someone. I want to keep it so special that I isolate it from the rest of the flow of life, and—" The bubble popped. "So now, the specialness has disappeared, but at least maybe I can hold on to the love itself ... " The water began to leak through her fingers and drip to the ground. No matter how hard she squeezed her fingers together, the water eventually leaked through. She placed her free hand underneath to stop the leaking. "Well, at least I will have some kind of love left over," she said, closing her hand into a fist. "The fear of losing any more causes me to squeeze even tighter." After a few more seconds, she opened her hands and showed them to Jonathan. They were almost completely dry. "You see? There is no more love left."

Jonathan blew air out from his cheeks and glanced at the pink ball; it was expanding. "You're talking about me, right?" He looked into her big brown eyes. "You're saying that I need to let you go for my own good?"

She tilted her head to one side and returned his look. "I am talking about any moment for any one. All of life is to be experienced. You and I need to jump back into the stream of life and rejoice and play and swim and dive and drink the beautiful water. That is the only way we can both move toward balance. Experience what you need for your lifetime—your learning experience—and do it with love. By doing that, we will become closer. The time is not far away when we will be back together again."

"I know," he said, "and I understand, intellectually. My heart doesn't understand, though. It hurts."

"Your heart does agree," she said, pointing at the pink ball. "The only reason it hurts is because of fear—fear of lost connection. Remember, my wonderful twin–flame, our hearts are always together. Always. Hopefully, that will take some of the sting out of the fear of loss which is nothing but an illusion. There is no real loss: we are together, always."

Jonathan nodded as though something just occurred to him. "All my Earth–life, I've been taught to fear that which is outside myself. Seeing myself as the source of disharmony is a hard concept to swallow all at once."

"But," Paula added, "knowing that you can create so much fear should be more than offset by the knowledge that you can create ten times more love by letting go!"

"You're right." He felt foolish. "I was even going to ask you now to be my special guide on Earth, but after thinking about it, I see that would have been just more fear in action, not love." He paused to consider what he'd just said. "Letting go ... it sure is hard, especially for an old fear–aholic like me. I love you a lot, my Paula ... "

He stopped talking because he could feel his throat getting dry and tight with emotion. He couldn't ever remember agreeing to stop seeing someone he loved so much, just because they asked him to.

"Old habits are hard to break, but for some strange reason, it sure feels good to let go," he said out loud. "Already, I feel freer."

"Yes!" she shouted. She jumped up and kissed him, full on the mouth. "You are so wonderful and I am so proud to be your twin–flame." She kissed him again. By now the pink energy field had enveloped both of them. "I told Ahmay and Ramda and Zorinthalian you could do it. You are awesome!" She kissed him again and again. "Do you realize what this means?"

"No. What?" he asked, completely bewildered.

"You have completed your first step toward becoming a teacher," she yelled, jumping for joy in his arms. "You are one in a million and you are my twin–flame." She bussed him on the cheek, nose, and forehead. "Yes! Yes! Yes!"

"Really?" he asked, scrambling to understand. "What am I teaching and to whom am I teaching it?"

"Yourself for now," she said. "Your own best teacher is always yourself. From now on, your job will to be to, first embrace and live the Universal Principles, and then finally share them with humankind. Remember, you teach best by example."

Suddenly the pink ball of light flickered and her eyes got big. "Oh, I guess it is time for you to go."

"What's going on?" he said.

"Just a couple of minutes until you are supposed to play for your audition."

"Oh, my God—I've got to go back to L.A.!" He panicked "How am I going to remember all the stuff I've learned? And I haven't even played the rest of my piece for you."

"Do not worry about remembering," she said. "It is all in your subconscious. Besides, you will not remember anything about your visit here when you wake up, at least not for a while. It will seem as if you fell asleep and had a dream, but cannot remember."

"What do you mean I won't remember? What good is all this if I can't remember?" His eyes widened. "I've got to go." He kissed her quickly on the lips and turned to run for the Celestial Bar.

"Where you going?" she asked, holding him from leaving. The pink light shrunk to the size of a soccer ball on her chest.

"I've got to go see Ramda."

"What for?"

"So he can help me memorize all the stuff I've learned. It may be only in my subconscious but I want to make sure I've got it right."

"Slow down, twin–flame," she said. "One thing at a time."

"What do you mean? You just told me I only had a couple of minutes. I have to say good–bye to Ahmay and the others."

"Chill out," she said, smiling. "All things in good time."

He rolled his eyes.

"Look, Jonathan, you are not leaving me until we properly lay this pink light to rest. Step back toward me and hold this ball with me."

He did. Both held the light; it was about four feet in diameter.

"Perfect," she said, "Now, put one hand over your heart and visualize a happy place on Earth where you would like to think of me, your twin–flame."

Jonathan thought of his favorite place to be alone in the middle of the night and watch the stars: way out on the very tip of the breakwater at the foot of Mission Beach in San Diego. That's where he felt the closest to all the forces of the universe. As he visualized that place, the pink ball of energy receded into both their hearts and disappeared.

"There," she said, sighing. "Now, you do not need to go see Ramda to memorize anything. You can do it right here and save all kinds of time."

"How can I do that?"

"Just use your intuition, Jonathan," she said. "Just focus on the beam of light and you can do the same thing he would."

"What? What are you talking about?"

"You are going to be a teacher. You have the same powers as Ramda. Just use them."

"I've never used them ... I don't know what I'm doing."

She closed her eyes, then opened them. "Four minutes, thirty seconds and counting," she said.

"All right. All right."

He used the technique of "looking beyond," just like he did when viewing the colors of his energy conduit centers. A fuzziness began in his peripheral vision and moved to the center. He then focused on his breath and visualized the Transition Room. Slowly the vision of the beam of light appeared.

"Welcome," boomed Ramda's deep voice.

"Excellent work, Young Bear," said Ahmay. "You learn well. You do us all proud. Outstanding work, Paula."

"I need to refresh my memory about all our lessons," Jonathan said. "I only have a few minutes."

The words were no sooner out of his mouth than a huge computer screen came into view. Across the top of the screen were the words:

Universal Principles

Underneath was the text:

EVERYTHING IS ENERGY
Love is the essence of all energy:
feel it in all that you do.

Energy Has VF
(vibrational frequencies)
Humankind's task is to raise theirs.

Energy Designs Form
Use it wisely.

Energy Must Move Freely
—like water downhill:
let it go.

Energy Is Limitless and Powerful
All you ever need is right before you.

ENERGY IS INTERCONNECTED
The universe is a Whole, comprised of
energies that interact, share, and create.

Energy Is a Reflection
To change the world, change yourself.

Energy Moves in a Circular Fashion
Be aware of all that you think, feel, and do—
it will come back to you a hundred–fold.

ENERGY JUST IS
Let go of all judgments and expectations:
you are perfect in this moment.

ENERGY IS MOVING
TOWARD BALANCE
Allow the Movement to stir you.
Know that you are of spirit reflected
in the physical, emotional, and
intellectual (PEIS).
Your task is to be in harmony with
yourself, with others, with your
planet, and with the Oneness.

Under the circles was the text:

THE HOW

Trust
Meditate
Go Within
Use Intuition
Feel LOVE in all things.
Remember you already know
The Universal Principles and The How.
People and events will trigger your remembrance.
Teach yourself first, then others by example, then by word.

"What is the matter, Young Bear?" asked Ahmay. "Do you not think you are up to the task?"

"I just didn't want to forget anything," he blurted.

"For you, it is not possible," Ramda interjected, "but I can understand your anxiety."

"Thanks for all your help," said Jonathan. "Sorry I'm in such a hurry. Hope I'll see you both again, real soon."

"You are welcome," Ramda and Ahmay chorused.

"Remember this computer is always here for you," added Ramda. "Beware of those cheap, earthly imitations!"

Four circles surrounded each of the Universal Principles. Jonathan could hear their chuckling as the circles became elliptical, and then connected:

"Watch for this special emblem," said Ahmay. "You will know we are close by."

The beam of light went blank in Jonathan's mind, and he blinked open both eyes.

Paula was still standing right beside him. "Four minutes, two seconds and counting," she monotoned, opening her eyes.

"Wow, that was fast," he said. "I've still got time to play a little of my concerto for you. Want to hear it?"

She bolted toward the bar. "I thought you would never ask," she yelled over her shoulder. "Last one there is a rotten egg!"

The couple took off running like two track stars. She barely beat him to the front door, and they rushed inside, jogging down the walkway between the booths toward the piano. She noticed that he was winded. "What is the matter, Taylor? Old age catching up with you?" she teased.

He smiled and kept going. When he got to the piano, he sat down on the stool and wiped his sweaty brow on the sleeves of his T–shirt. He paused for a few seconds to collect his thoughts.

Paula slid in beside him on the stool and kissed him softly on the cheek. "I love you, twin–flame," she whispered. "Do not ever forget that you are loved."

He turned to face her. He returned her kiss on the cheek. "Me, too, you," he said, staring deep into her eyes. "This is for you, with all my love."

He began to play the transition from the first to the second movement. He felt his soul soaring, exactly as it did when Ahmay took him on the "eagle" trip while they were sitting in a booth. He closed his eyes and he felt like an eagle. He saw himself soaring again, high up in the air. There was someone with him. He looked over and it was Paula. Their wings almost touched. Tears came to his eyes, and he didn't care. This was where they belonged—soaring and gliding with the Four Winds.

Jonathan felt the music pouring from his soul. It was different this time. He had never played like this before; this was the best. But he hadn't gotten to the hard spot yet. Never mind, he told himself; let yourself soar. Let the winds blow. Glide and let the energy flow. He was getting close to the part where his finger always cramped. Just keep going, Taylor. Let all the energy move through you without any blockages. You're almost there—just a couple more bars.

He felt his right hand getting warm, especially his finger. He opened his eyes. Paula had moved her right hand to less than an inch above his. He closed his eyes again. His hand felt fine. He was going to do it. He was going to soar and play the whole piece like he had never played it before in his whole life. One more bar to go ...

A loud knocking exploded in Digger's head. There it went again. "Mr. Taylor," said a loud, gruff voice. "Mr. Taylor, if you hear me, just answer something."

Digger shook his head and blinked open his eyes. "Okay, okay," he muttered in a groggy voice. "I hear you."

"Fifteen minutes till your audition, sir," said a faintly familiar voice. "Are you all right?"

Digger felt a strange warmth in his right hand. He flexed it and kept trying to clear away the cobwebs from his mind. "Yeah, I'm fine," he croaked. "Must have fallen sound asleep. I'll be fine. Thanks for waking me."

"I'll be back in ten minutes to make sure you're all right," said the same voice. It sounded like the guard who'd brought him in.

Digger felt strangely tired, like he'd been drugged or something. He'd never experienced a meditation like that before. He wiped his eyes. They felt like he had been crying. Funny. I can't remember having any dreams. Why would I be crying during a meditation? I feel pretty good. Why would I be crying?

You'd better get it together, Taylor. You're almost out of time. Your big opportunity is about to happen.

Wonder what's happened to my hand? Maybe I slept on it or something. Maybe my finger healed while I was sleeping.

There you go again—wishing for the impossible.

He got up from the couch and walked over to the warm–up piano. He took a deep breath and sat down.

Chapter 13

" ... feel the truth."

Digger looked around the dressing room from the stool of the shiny baby grand. Nothing appeared to have changed while he was asleep. It was the biggest and best-looking dressing room Digger had ever seen. He still couldn't get over the ash paneling, the expensive furniture and flowers—even a stocked wet bar.

He looked at his watch: 7:19. Everything was on schedule. He'd just warm up for a couple of minutes before putting on his tux. He remembered Sean Green's last words: "Best bib and tucker." Wonder if he's out there? Surprising that he would send a car to pick me up and not even send a note or howdy message or anything. Sure is a strange character.

Digger scowled. Out of nowhere, he felt that same sense of foreboding that had been coming and going all day. You've got to stop these negative thoughts, he told himself. It doesn't matter where these stupid negative vibrations are coming from, you've got to put them out of your head. There's not a damn thing you can do about them, so just concentrate on the task ahead. You've got a concerto to play in just a few minutes.

He looked at his right hand again. The warm feeling was gone. It felt just fine. He shook his hands to loosen them up and then began to play. Given the limited time, he thought he'd pick up the music just before the transition from the first to the second movement.

As he played, he tried to improve his frame of mind by thinking about the happier times in his life. The first thing that popped into his head was a fishing trip with his dad. He was ten years old, and it was just the two of them. One whole day alone with his dad. No mother to stir things up. No telephone to take Pop back to work. No list of chores that had to be done because they just "needed doing," as he used to tell Digger. Just the two of them, all alone on a quiet lake, fishing for trout.

It was the middle of summer, yet for some strange reason it was a gray, cool day. Actually, it was the kind of day Digger loved. He hated the oppressive, muggy summers of Chicago. They made him think he was in Hell without having had all the fun it took to get there. Shawano Lake was a three–hour drive from the Taylor family home, but it might as well have been on another planet: no traffic, no airplanes roaring around up above, and none of the rude and hysterical behavior by adults that was a part of Digger's everyday life in the city.

Pop had packed a double lunch and snack for the two of them and they just sat there in the boat for hours, not saying a word—just casting, reeling in the line jerky–like, a little at a time, and eating as much as they wanted, whenever they wanted. It was like being set free from jail and he was with his dad, safe and protected. Nothing could go wrong. It was one of the best days of his life.

Digger was getting close to the tricky spot in the music. His finger felt fine; nothing special. He'd certainly slept a long time. Wonder what those tears were all about? Not like you to cry, especially in your sleep. Wonder why I can't remember where I was when I was meditating? Seems like I was in a dream. Dreams sure are strange—sometimes you remember them and sometimes you don't. It felt as if something important happened, but what was it?

Almost to the moment of truth with the music. It reminded him of watching Olympic figure skating: would she do the triple Lutz or not? Would he be able to play through his moment of hesitation? Would his finger perform? Would he be able to find the musical freedom and soar to new heights? He'd know in a moment.

A loud knock on the door interrupted him. "Mr. Taylor? Mr. Taylor, can you hear me?" Digger stopped playing.

"Yeah," he said. Slowly he stood, walked to the door, and opened it.

Still dressed in his gray uniform with gold trim, the security guard stood just outside the door, looking at his watch. "You've got about five minutes, sir."

"Thanks," said Digger, starting to close the door.

The guard saw that Digger had only shorts and a tennis shirt on. "Excuse me, sir," said the guard. "You're not going out there like that are you?"

"I've got to change yet."

"Oh," said the guard. "Well ... break-a-leg and all that stuff."

Digger started to close the door again.

"I heard you playing, sir," said the guard. "Sounds pretty good to me. Not too shabby for a musician who's never had his own dressing room."

Digger chuckled and smiled. "Thanks. You've got a good memory. I've got to go now, okay?"

"Right. See ya later."

Digger closed the door and looked at his watch again: 7:26. Four minutes to get your tux on and get your head together. Sweet mother of pearl, and you haven't even given your piece a name yet! Come on, Taylor. Get your head in the game.

At precisely 7:30 p.m., Jonathan Taylor—Digger to his friends and acquaintances—emerged from his dressing room, immaculately attired in a rented tux. He walked quickly down the corridor to the steps and the entry door Mr. White had instructed him to use. He took a deep breath and opened the stage door. Let's do it, Taylor, he told himself. Let's make Mother proud. He stopped for a moment and switched gears in his head. Let's make *me* proud.

As he opened the door, he spotted TV camera operators and boomed mikes on stage as well as just in front of the stage. House spots and floodlights glared down onto the red curtain and the two black keyboard instruments that awaited him. He marched to the side of the Steinway and bowed to the audience. He couldn't see who was out there because of the lights.

"Good evening, ladies and gentlemen," he said, his voice clear and crisp. "My name is Jonathan Taylor. Tonight, I'd like to play a special piece for you. It's a piano concerto in two movements entitled"—he hesitated—"Piano Concerto in D."

Polite applause greeted his announcement while he slid onto the piano stool and made himself comfortable. It seemed as if there were more people out there than he'd expected—sounded like fifty people clapping.

This is it, Taylor. This is what you've been hoping for—for who knows how long? Seems like forever. Three years can seem like the blink of an eye and an eternity all at the same time.

Digger rubbed his hands together.

This was the magical moment. But he was fighting anxiety about the phrases in the transition section and about his finger—his fears lurked in the shadows of his mind, hoping to distract him. He was also fighting off a natural fear of screwing up—that'd he'd blow it and ruin any chance he ever had of making a new career for himself. And then there was that feeling of impending doom. He had to dismiss that from his mind; he'd deal with it later, after the audition. He couldn't do anything about it now.

All that flashed through his mind in a millisecond.

None of that negative stuff's going to do you any good right now, Taylor, he told himself. You've got to try something different. The big question is, what? What can you do at this moment that is different and still has a chance for better results than anything you've ever done before? It'll come to you. Start playing, with feeling.

Digger began to play.

Keep it light, buddy. Nice and light and gentle. Sad but gentle, not maudlin.

His thoughts turned to his father again.

There you were, Pop, at the funeral home. You were really dead, all white–faced and still as a picture on a wall. Impossible for me to believe that you were never going to be there again for me, your college graduate son. We were going to be such good friends, you and I, if only you would have let me in. You were going to come visit when I got married. Later, when I was older, I was going to make you a grandfather. You would have made a wonderful grandpa, but now it would never be. You were dead. Really dead.

Digger's touch was light upon the keyboard, fingers springing key to key with the grace and strength of a ballet dancer's legs.

His thoughts drifted back to their vacation in Key West: Digger talking to his dad about drinking himself to death, and his dad's reply, "I know exactly what I'm doing."

He felt himself giving in to the conflict his father's passing had created—emotions he'd seldom allowed himself to feel. He felt guilty for his father's death. He'd wanted to tell him that he loved him that day in Key West, that he would miss him terribly if he wasn't around. But he hadn't. He didn't do or say anything. He just stood there—holding back his thoughts and his emotions. If only he'd said those things, maybe his father would have stopped drinking.

That was the day Digger truly started to build new walls around his heart—walls that music had once broken down. He built them stronger and higher so that this time, not a drop of music could leak through. His biggest fear had been of drowning—drowning from the tidal wave of emotions, should the dam ever break. Digger was afraid of his anger, anger he couldn't admit feeling toward his father for his total disregard for everyone else when he decided to die.

You went off and left me with Mom, Digger thought now, as his fingers flew over the keys. That wasn't fair. And she was mad at you, too, and took it all out on me. Why did you have to do that? Why did you have to leave me alone with her and all her anger? I didn't know how to distinguish between anger and parents and dying. I didn't know anything. I just knew that she spent most days screaming at me for nothing and there wasn't anything I could do about it. She was my only parent. I couldn't fire her. I had to keep quiet, but I didn't like it, not one damn bit. But why am I laying all this on you, Pop? You were dead.

Good grief, Taylor. Why are you beating up on your dead father? Nerves, probably. Reliving all those childhood feelings that you were always afraid to air. But why now? You've had twenty years to do this. Why now, in the middle of this important moment, are you resurrecting old wounds? Well, you've succeeded in one thing: this is certainly a different way to handle an audition. Not what I had in mind, though.

Digger was just coming to the end of the first movement. His fingers were still filled with confidence and energy. He felt better than he had in years, allowing himself to feel all those emotions he'd been so afraid of. He wasn't a bad person for having them, he realized now. He was finally being honest with himself.

The issue wasn't really his dad but him: his inability to feel all that he could; his inability to share those feelings, whatever they might be—anger or happiness, sadness or excitement, love or hate. His inability to confront his father's passiveness and his mother's aggressiveness. His fear of allowing Mary's love into his life because that might unlock the reservoir of emotions dammed up inside of him.

That was the key; that's what made him feel so much better. It was the freedom to tell the truth. The freedom to feel the truth. That was it: to *feel* the truth.

Digger opened his eyes for a brief second to make sure he wasn't dreaming. He saw the red curtain and the blazing spotlights. In one corner of the stage, his eye caught a glimpse of American and California flags, side–by–side. At the top of each wooden flagpole was the emblem of an eagle. He closed his eyes again. That was it: he would soar like an eagle, just like he did sometimes in his dreams.

His heart jumped for joy. This was it. He was going to do it. His concerto was going to fly. He was going to let himself go and feel the truth, the truth about his father and his mother and himself and his life and everything else. He didn't have to lie anymore or pretend. It was all in there, inside himself. He could fly and soar just like an eagle.

He was coming to the part where he always messed up. He didn't care; it didn't matter. It wasn't a problem. He was going to soar right through it, like an eagle soaring through a down draft.

Suddenly, his right hand began to get warm again and he felt as if he had powers within him he'd never dreamed of. He was re–writing his concerto as he played; the music he played was better than anything he'd ever written. He'd found the passion. It was truth—the truth about the way he really felt about everything. He was free!

His fingers raced over the keyboard, inventing new themes, finding new harmonies and counterpoints, introducing new melodic interlines. Who was this guy playing the piano? Was it really him? This music had been inside him all these years, trying to get out. All these months and years, he had heard this concerto in his head, but hadn't been able to get it out. Now that it was flowing, he didn't want it to stop.

He flew right by the part in the transition that had plagued him for months, ever since the softball accident. It was as if there had never been a problem. His right hand was still warm and feeling strong.

Whatever you do, Taylor, don't think about what you're doing. Just let the music and passion flow. Think loving thoughts; no more negative thoughts for you. No more blame game. Pop didn't do anything to you; you did it to yourself, and Mom wasn't mean to you on purpose. It just happened. They both loved you the best they could. They were just people learning from their life experiences. Just like you have learned from them. They made mistakes, just like you have. What happened in Florida wasn't anyone's fault—it simply happened. There were lessons to be learned out there about how you could be a better human being, Taylor. Oh, let it flow, Jonathan Patrick Taylor. Go ahead and soar like an eagle! See yourself high above the earth. Look down below. The problems of the world are so small and insignificant when you're up here and gliding on the wind. It's the love you give that matters.

He wanted to look side–to–side to see if he was alone. He had the strange feeling there were others up here with him, but he was afraid that, if he looked, he might forget how to fly and then he would crash. He had almost finished playing the second movement. It was the best he'd ever played it, he knew that, but he didn't want to think about it. Instead, he continued to enjoy the release of his emotions moving magically through his fingers into the stringed instrument. And as a reward, the notes not only came back to him as sound to his ears but as a reverberation felt in every cell of his body. It was a joyous reunion of the music he had always heard in his head, and the outward expression of this remembrance.

The music was perfectly balanced. Digger felt like he was moving towards a blissful state, with his body as the instrument for this relationship between mind and heart. Now something stirred deep within him. Something that the currents of the deep ocean had finally uncovered. It moved slowly up towards the surface. Still too deep to know what it was—but it was coming.

And suddenly he was done. He struck the last chord, paused for effect, and then stood for what he thought would be modest or, at the very best, polite applause from whoever had managed to stay awake through the whole concerto.

You shouldn't have come, he thought. You're not a movie score composer. Well, it's not a total loss. At least now you know what you've got to do to get the best out of whatever talent God has given you.

As he bowed to the audience, thunderous applause erupted from the theater. He felt as if he were being overrun by a tidal wave of cheers and shouts of "Encore!"

One loud male voice seemed to stand out. "Come on, Taylor," it bellowed with sarcasm, "play us some more. Play us another concerto, just one movement—that's all we ask."

A pang of fright shot through Digger. What if they kept clapping and cheering? He wasn't prepared to play anything else; he could have planned something, but it never occurred to him. Sean Green hadn't said anything about a second piece.

Suddenly Mr. White was standing by him. "Come on, let's get you outta here."

They went out the stage door, down the steps, and into Digger's dressing room.

"You did all right," the guard blurted, slamming the door shut and locking it.

"Thanks," Digger said, winded and scowling. "Why'd you lock that door? I want people to be able to come see me if they want. I'm expecting a visitor."

The guard smiled and took off his cap. "First of all, let me introduce myself. My name is really Philip Michaelson." He extended his hand.

Digger stared at the man's hand and finally took it. "I'm happy to shake your hand, whoever you are," he said, smiling at his own naiveté, "but you're going to have to talk awfully long and awfully hard to convince me that you're really Mr. Michaelson, the director."

The man smiled again. "I like that. You handled that well." He reached inside his trousers and pulled out his wallet and credit cards. He handed them all to Digger. "Feel free to inspect anything in there you want," he said, checking his appearance in the mirrors over the dressing table. "If you're still unsure about who I am, we can make a few phone calls. Believe me when I tell you, I really am who I say I am."

Digger examined the wallet and its contents. He found a driver's license with Philip Michaelson's name and picture on it. They matched this man's appearance. "It looks like you really are Philip Michaelson," he finally muttered, shaking his head. "Why did you impersonate someone else?"

As he handed the wallet back to Michaelson, a faint feeling of impending danger approaching from the theater flashed through Digger's consciousness.

"I like to get to know people without their knowing who I am," Michaelson said, making himself comfortable on one of the couches. "People usually get nervous and uptight when they know who I am."

He gestured for Digger to sit down. The silver–haired director brushed back his hair with one hand and studied his visitor. "That was an inspiring piece you spun for us out there, Mr. Taylor. As you could tell, my staff and crew kind of liked it, too." He paused to rub his chin. "Actually, I'm told you prefer to be called Digger. That so?"

The younger man nodded. "It's from my baseball days."

"Well anyway, Digger," he said, smiling and giving affected emphasis to the nickname, "what do you think? Want to make a movie with this crazy, crotchety old curmudgeon?"

Digger's head was awhirl. Was Philip Michaelson actually offering him the job? As Michaelson went on to describe the film, Digger wondered if he'd lose the job if he asked if they could talk tomorrow. Right now, his mind felt like nothing more than a mass of amorphous tissue. He needed sleep.

As if he'd heard Digger's thought, Michaelson stood up from the couch. "I can see I've given you too much to think about already. Please excuse this passionate old man, Digger. I haven't even given you a chance to change out of your tux. This must be pretty overwhelming."

Digger stood also. "That's all right, Mr. Michaelson. I want to hear more. But I do need some fresh air and a good night's sleep. Can we talk tomorrow?"

"Don't worry about that," said Michaelson, heading for the door. "I know you're going to have to get your life reorganized a bit before I can expect to see you every day. But you went on the payroll the minute you walked on stage tonight. Sure glad we taped your performance; it was brilliant! You were brilliant. Can't believe you've been hiding yourself down in San Diego." He paused. "We'll definitely talk tomorrow."

Digger beamed. "Thank you, Mr. Michaelson. I ... I don't know what else to say."

"When you don't know what to say," the director grinned, "it's usually best to do like my mother told my sister for her first prom: 'Keep everything closed 'cept your ears and your nose.'" He roared at his own joke and opened the door, "When you're ready to leave, there will be a driver waiting downstairs. He'll take you to the Beverly Hilton, where you'll be my guest. We're having a surprise party at Spago for one of the film's producers. If you'd like to come, tell the driver to pick you up later. I'll be at the party to introduce you around. And how about breakfast? I'll send my driver, say at six. That too early?"

Digger smiled. "What if I say yes?"

Michaelson shrugged. "Nothing; I'll just send him later. Name the time."

"Six is fine." Digger blushed. He'd been testing Michaelson—unfairly, he realized. "I like getting up early, especially when it's to write music and get paid for it."

"Good." Michaelson extended his hand and they shook. "Then it's all settled. Goodnight and welcome aboard! We're going to make a great movie together. You'll see." He disappeared down the corridor.

Digger turned back into the dressing room, leaving the door slightly open. "Yes!" he exclaimed in a loud whisper, punching the air. "Yes, yes!" He punched at the air again and again. "Good God, Almighty," he muttered. "Can you believe it?" He plopped himself onto the couch and then lay down, kicking his feet into the air. "Yesterday a waiter, tomorrow a movie score composer! Taylor, can you believe it?" He wanted to share the news and tell someone—but who? His mother? Mary?

He suddenly felt the effects of the exhausting day. So much excitement and hardly a wink of sleep in the last thirty-six hours. He let out a long sigh and closed his eyes.

A cold chill moved through him. And again. It filled the room—that feeling that something horrible was about to happen, stronger than ever.

What's going on with you, Taylor? Are you losing it? It's like you're determined to ruin your own enjoyment of life. You've just hit the ball out of the park and now you start this same old doom and gloom crap.

Someone knocked on the door.

"Who is it?" Digger called out.

"Patrick, me boy," answered a familiar voice, "ya got time to see an old friend, have ya?"

The "something bad" got worse. Fear clutched Digger's stomach. Why? He thought about telling Green to go away, but that was crazy. How could he tell Green to go away? He was the one who made it all happen.

Green breezed in with a cherubic smile like he owned the place. His clothes were impeccable. Not a hair was out of order. He looked to be about 45, handsome, with strong determined features. "Will ya look at this?" he said, giving the room a fleeting once-over. He extended his hand to Digger. "'Bout time ya crawled out from under yer rock in San Diego, ya know. Nice to me'chya, lad."

Digger took Green's hand and his fear deepened. Something was very much amiss. He needed to get out of there, and fast.

"Nice to meet you, too, Mr. Green." Better postpone any business until tomorrow, Taylor. There's something fishy about this guy. "But I've got to hurry and change out of this tux. Someone's waiting for me."

"Quite all right, lad." Green headed for the bar. "You go ahead and change; I'll fix us a drink to celebrate. Ya know ya knocked 'em dead tonight, don't chya?"

"No drinks for me, thanks," Digger said. "It would knock me on my keister right now."

How could he get rid of this man politely? I've got to get this monkey suit off and get out of here. Something's wrong with this guy. There's a manner about him. Reminds me of someone I've seen someplace before.

As Digger sat at the dressing table, he could see Green behind him, reflected in the mirror. Another mirror behind the wet bar showed Digger everything Green was doing as he rummaged among the bottles beneath the bar.

"Oh, go on, lad. Ya've got to celebrate a little. It isn't every day ya fool the likes a' Philip Michaelson, ya know. He thinks yer the Second Coming."

Digger frowned. "Fooled? What are you talking about?"

"Well, lad, we both know about yer trouble with the transition and yer bad pinkie, now don't we? Some kinda miracle ya pulled out there on stage, dazzlin' em with yer footwork 'n all."

Digger didn't know what to say. This was strange talk from someone who was supposed to be his agent and advocate. Digger stared intensely at Green's reflection in the mirror. It became a little fuzzy. For a moment he thought he saw another face superimposed over Green's.

Digger remembered a trick that he'd seen people use to view camouflaged three-dimensional pictures. He'd used that technique lately, but he couldn't remember where. He focused his gaze on the outside perimeter of Green's reflection and then he froze. He didn't want to move his head; he just kept it at the same angle. Who was that image in the mirror?

The reflection became clearer and looked vaguely familiar. The reflected image was a man about Digger's age, dressed in black, holding a tray full of bar glasses. It then began to change—now he saw that it was the man who beat him and threw him through the window—the attacker who always appeared in his nightmares.

Digger was stunned by the images in front of him as he heard Green sing:

"Aren't ya tired of runn'n from the devil? Don't ya know, he's just like you and me."

Hearing the ballad intensified Digger's fear and he lost his focus. The image changed back into Green's.

"Ya been a tough guy to find, Patrick. But eventually ya'd always let me know where ya were."

"What are you talking about?"

Ignoring Digger's question, he laughed. "You've always believed that I'm the one who's responsible."

Fear pulsed through Digger's body like so many other times in his life—that weekend in Chicago, the night the restaurant sank, but especially lately: when he broke his finger at the softball game, on the Mission Beach jetty, when he was in the limo, when he'd gotten calls from Green.

"Ya know ya never can get rid a' me. I'm really yer friend and here to help ya. But it's been fun tormentin' ya."

Digger took a deep breath and heard the words "Let Go" in his mind. He concentrated again on using the technique.

"Now yer different. Ya never would allow yerself to see me before now. Do ya think ya can handle it, me boy?"

Green's face grew blurry: it wasn't the talent agent's face anymore. The new image was now becoming clearer—all too clear. Digger didn't want to believe it. Goosebumps covered his entire body.

It was Digger's own face.

Digger got up from the dressing table, but his knees were wobbly. He made it to the couch, collapsing and covering his face with his hands. He wanted to get the hell out of there. Something bizarre was happening and he didn't have the time or the energy to figure it all out. Suddenly, he felt his right hand get warm and he remembered how he'd felt at the piano on stage. He remembered how good it felt to fly like an eagle.

That was it: the truth. The truth had set him free: the truth of his feelings had allowed him to soar to new heights. He wasn't going to run away from this menace. Whoever or whatever Green was, Digger had to find out once and for all. He was tired of either building walls against or running away from his fears. Enough is enough. He had to finally confront this person. Whoever he was. Whatever it took. In spite of the fear he felt, he was ready to face … whomever. He removed his hands from his face and opened his eyes.

The dressing room was empty except for Digger. The door was still slightly ajar. Green had vanished into thin air. Digger got up from the couch and walked to the bar. Two glasses had been used recently to mix drinks. Did Michaelson do that, or did Green, or did I and, because of my lack of sleep, don't remember? Is this room just a giant dream? Is this whole trip nothing but a dream?

There was a loud knock on the open door.

Digger didn't answer.

"Mr. Taylor," yelled a strong male voice.

What in the world is going on now? he wondered. Is this some kind of trick by Green or something? Maybe he's a magician and he's just messing with my mind to make some kind of point? If it is Green, nothing's changed. The truth will set me free. Whatever he's got to dish out, I can handle. "Come on in."

A man poked his head through the door. "I'm Johnson with building security. I have a note for you that someone left at my station."

Digger went over and took the note. "Did you see the man who wrote this?"

"Nope. Just saw it a second ago lying on my desk." The security guard started to walk away, then turned and said, "Don't mean to rush you, but I'm locking everything up in just a few minutes."

"Thanks. I'll be out of here real soon."

Digger closed the door and looked at his name printed on the folded piece of paper: *Jonathan Patrick Taylor*

He opened the note.

Sorry I couldn't stay. I'll meet with you at another time and another place.

S. Green

He was too tired to think anymore. He just wanted to get out of there. Digger quickly changed and packed. He hurried down the steps to find a long white limo waiting for him, a male driver by its front door. Digger took a deep breath and looked up into the clear night sky. The stars appeared to be shining more brightly than usual. He smiled and watched the heavens for a moment. His right hand started to get warm again. He took it from his pocket to look at and something fell out onto the steps. He stooped to pick it up. It was the envelope Mary had given him at Ocean Beach—what seemed like a year ago, but it had only been early that morning.

He got into the rear of the limo and dialed Mary's new number.

"Hello?" she said, groggily.

"Hi there. I didn't wake you, did I?"

"Well, hello." Her voice sprang to life. "You sound ... far away. Where are you?"

"In L.A. ... It's a long story. I'll tell you about it in just a sec. First, I have a question," he said, finding the switch and rolling back the skylight. For some reason, he wanted to watch the stars as they spoke. "You think our flower is still alive and healthy?"

About the Author

Tom Youngholm grew up on the south side of Chicago and graduated with a B.A. in Communication and an M.A. in Human Relations. His professional careers have included: family counselor and public educator for the Cook County Sheriff's Youth Services Department in Chicago; owner of a floating seafood restaurant in the Florida Keys, Training Specialist for General Dynamics in Professional Development, and corporate consultant.

He loves playing the piano and enjoys all sports. He has been in community theater, as well as a few professional productions.

"As I was approaching forty and went to the Celestial Bar, I finally found out what I was supposed to be doing when I grew up——TEACHING."

The Quest

I Hang In The Balance
   Not Aware That I Created It

I Am The Balance
   Afraid To Fall Into The Unknown

I Am The Unknown
   Not Aware That I Know

I Am The Creating

                    The Falling

                          The Knowing

So I Let Myself Fall

   That I May Know

   And In Knowing Be Creative

So Here I Am Hanging In The Balance

                          AGAIN